Shannon Thomas is a Florida native and graduate of the University of Florida. She also holds degrees from Clemson University and the University of South Florida. She grew up in Gainesville, FL, and has attended her fair share of Gator football games. Writing has long been a passion and creative outlet.

Shannon Thomas

THE FAMILY

AUSTIN MACAULEY PUBLISHERS™
LONDON • CAMBRIDGE • NEW YORK • SHARJAH

Ordering Information
Quantity sales: Special discounts are available on quantity purchases by corporations, associations, and others. For details, contact the publisher at the address below.

Publisher's Cataloging-in-Publication data
Thomas, Shannon
The Family

ISBN 9781638296478 (Paperback)
ISBN 9781638296485 (ePub e-book)

Library of Congress Control Number: 2023915657

www.austinmacauley.com/us

First Published 2023
Austin Macauley Publishers LLC
40 Wall Street, 33rd Floor, Suite 3302
New York, NY 10005
USA

mail-usa@austinmacauley.com
+1 (646) 5125767

Chapter One

The leaves had fallen from the trees and the thick gray clouds over the estate brought a sense of acceptance to the coming winter. The sun refused to show its face, but small rays could be seen attempting to peak through. The temperature had an icy bite to it that would inevitably herald snow within the next few days. The view from the concrete balcony overlooked the five hundred acres of season changing trees and open land behind the Skyler estate. The family had once thought of dispersing the property, but then mysteriously reconsidered and made it the family seat instead of the vacation home.

Hidden away in the back woods of Oregon lies the estate of Frederick Skyler. His family was one of the initial settlers to Oregon at its statehood in the mid-nineteenth century. To this end, the family had been involved in the grain industry since its inception to the state. Mr. Skyler constantly kept an eye on his business interests. Mrs. Skyler had never seen, to anyone's knowledge, a person, or business that was not Fifth Avenue oriented in some form or fashion. The public fascination with the family extended as far back as their settlement to the state. Their home was subject to rumors and gossip in town.

The two awoke each morning in their master bedroom on the third floor. The house was built upon and made structurally sound by stone and throughout the generations had been maintained by the very same. Plastic overlay had been applied to the wallpaper decades ago, all over the estate walls, to prevent the paper from crumpling and decaying. As a result, the rooms began to look more pristine and at the same time, the estate resembled more of a museum than a home.

The Skyler's were very habitual. Each morning they rose, and Patricia would use her dressing room and her maid would assist her with whatever attire she would be wearing that day. Frederick would follow the same routine, but after he had partaken of a decent breakfast on the balcony overlooking the back of the estate. On this day, Patricia delayed her normal rush to organize. She walked down the hall lined with portraits of her husband's ancestors stopping every so often to run her finger along one or two that she deemed worthy of cleaning. The portraits were hung from wires that were pinned beneath the crown molding.

Patricia turned and resumed her walk down the hall as staff began opening the drapes to let the sunshine into the home. Patricia adjusted her engraved bracelet and looked twice in the mirror to check her appearance before finally turning the corner and was surprised by the newest maid: Rachel. "Good morning, Mrs. Skyler," said Rachel. Rachel's job was to vacuum the rugs and dust the furnishings in the rooms on the second floor. Mrs. Skyler was pondering her presence on the residential floor when Rachel asked a question.

"Mrs. Skyler, I was wondering if I could switch my workdays from early morning to midafternoon? I know that Wendy usually handles these matters, but I thought after working here for a month I could—" And with that, she stopped. Patricia had simply looked at her with that piercing glare she was known to give her employees when they had crossed a line. Rachel had been hired after long time staff member, Grace, had resigned late last month and had learned most of the regular goings on within the walls. Grace had been with the family since anyone could remember. She had helped to perfect the Skyler system of operation within the walls. Following her breast cancer diagnosis, she resigned and chose to live out her last weeks on her own terms. On the night she passed away, Frederick seemed quite unhinged.

From the in-laws' suite adjacent to the balcony, came Richard. Richie was a man of medium build, in his late forties, and by all accounts the second hardest working member of the staff since Grace's death. The three of them stood beside the open wood paneled doors leading to the rear balcony where Frederick was quietly sipping his coffee. Richie began speaking with apologies on behalf of Rachel almost immediately. He had overheard the conversation as he was making up the bed in the in-laws' suite. He knew what was coming and decided to have a quiet aside with Rachel, but as he stepped across the drawing room, he saw the look on Mrs. Skyler's face and saw that something was wrong and it had nothing to do with Rachel.

"I am terribly sorry, ma'am," he said. "Rachel, is it? I am sure we can go and speak to Wendy about any scheduling queries you may have." He glanced at Mrs.

Skyler and she exhaled and looked at Richie and nodded. He glanced at Rachel and she began to blush at once acknowledging her error. She began to utter apologies to Richie about her behavior as quietly as she could and he was trying to calm her poor nerves because she had never before addressed Mrs. Skyler and did not know what had possessed her to do so today.

Just as they were crossing the drawing room for the stairs outside the double doors, Mrs. Skyler stated, "Please inform the staff this morning that Junior, Patty, and Greg are coming this weekend for a visit."

The two employees stopped in their tracks, looked at each other and turned very slowly to face Mrs. Skyler and said, "Yes, ma'am." They exited the room through the intricately carved oak doors and descended the winding stairs for the first floor. Once there they made their way to Wendy's office.

The room was completely white from the ceiling above to the walls surrounding and the floor beneath. The windows laid into the highest point of the northern wall provided a view of the tumultuous gray sky above and green grass immediately outside it. The office was fifteen feet wide and fifteen feet long. There were three clocks in the room mounted side by side on the western wall. One clock was for Oregon, the next for New York and the final one for England. Each clock was round with antique block numbers and black borders. The only person permitted to adjust them was Wendy.

The office had a mahogany desk that was planted in front of the northern wall with three metal baskets evenly spaced apart lying on it. The basket on the far right of the desk contained monthly work schedules, the middle for special assignments such as charity dinner schedules, security changes, and requests for one-on-one meetings with Wendy and finally the last was reserved for the children of the Skyler's. It remained empty on a regular basis. Richie and Rachel walked into the planning office and found Wendy adjusting the clocks. Her back was turned to the duo.

"Wendy" stated Richard.

"Hmm?" She turned and observed the caution in Rachel's face and the sideways glance that Richie had given in Rachel's direction. She took a deep breath and placed England's clock back in its place on the wall. She took a few steps toward Richie and Rachel and held her hands together in front of her. Richie began regaling her with the situation and was stopped when he reached the change in schedule point. Wendy held up her right hand for him to stop. She looked at Rachel and gestured with her right hand toward the baskets on the table.

"Are you familiar with the baskets and their purpose to employees old and new?" she asked Rachel.

"Yes," she responded glumly. "I don't know why I didn't just put in for a meeting with you, but logically I was in the drawing room across from the stairs leading to the residential floor. I reasoned that it would be more time effective to ask Mrs. Skyler this morning about the change in my work schedule than to wait until my shift was over today to schedule a meeting with you." After finishing her explanation, she merely shrugged. Rachel was a 27-year-old experienced household worker. She came to the estate with excellent references and was immediately hired. No one simply arrived at the entry driveway gates. Everyone that had ever applied to the household had been drawn there. The fact was that every employee inside the walls and managing the acres of land had three things in common: they had no family, excellent work experience and were exceedingly loyal. The last attribute was something the Skyler's valued above all. Wendy furrowed her eyebrows together.

"Did anything out of the ordinary happen today?" Wendy asked Richard. He stared at Wendy for a few seconds and finally cleared his throat. He and Rachel looked at each other for a moment.

"Mrs. Skyler asked me to inform the staff that Junior, Patty, and Greg are coming this weekend for a visit," he said.

Wendy blinked, cleared her throat, looked to Rachel, and said, "We'll speak about your scheduling paradox tomorrow morning at 8:30 sharp." Rachel sighed, made apologies, and left to resume her work for the day. Wendy looked at Richie and walked out of the office. Richie soon followed after her. As Wendy and Richie proceeded down the long corridor to the security offices one floor below, Mrs. Skyler proceeded to walk out to the balcony to breakfast with Mr. Skyler.

"Good morning, Trish," he said as he took a sip of coffee and placed it back on its saucer. Patricia took her customary seat opposite him at the black oval table. The table was set for two that morning as Patricia had requested the previous evening. The table had a glass covering its black iron top to protect the intricate floral vine detailing beneath. The plates were white with genuine gold borders and floral embossing just beneath.

"Good morning, Fred." Patricia began to eat while Frederick read The Times. After Patricia had sipped her coffee for the second time, she spoke.

"Rick phoned last night while you were at the office," she said casually. Mr. Skyler cleared his throat, walked to the wall of the balcony and looked over the property lost in thought. He took a sip from the cup and exhaled. From the balcony, he could just make out the black roof of the Skyler cabin. The tree line refused to show anymore beyond the roof, but he knew what was there. The mirror lake lay just beyond the cabin encircled by gargantuan red oaks with next to no light hitting it. Apart from the rays from the sun and moon, the lake was completely invisible from the balcony of the estate. He took a deep breath and exhaled.

"How is Rick?" he asked.

"He said that the three of them are coming this weekend for a visit. They've booked a flight for tomorrow morning and should be here around midnight," Trish stated. She was excited that the children were coming home especially in time for the charity gala. Fred simply nodded with his back to Trish and continued to stare out over the tree line lost in thought. He turned to Trish and leaned against the wall of the balcony.

"Does Wendy know? Is Rick still upset? How's Patty? Greg should be finishing up with the search in New York," he said.

"Perhaps we can convince them to stay the month. It has been so long since we were together as a family and not as a 'philanthropic organization'." She was eyeing the paper that Mr. Skyler had placed on the table and had read aloud from a headline discussing the upcoming annual charity gala at the Skyler estate.

"I am sure he will be found soon, but in the meantime, we cannot go on like this. I want the boys and Patty back home for more than just a quick visit. Rick seems less agitated, but at least he called. I haven't heard from my babies in a month. He said Patty had worse luck than Greg and he combined searching for him. I told Richie about the kids coming this weekend, so Wendy knows. I'm sure she's just as anxious to see them as we are. Albeit the staff's last encounter with the five of us together was tenser than I would have liked but given the circumstances I can't blame Rick for being upset and Greg has learned to control is temper after all this time. Think of what would have happened if the two of them had gone to the hospital. Patty knew it was impossible. She understands how it works," she said. He nodded and calmly replied.

"The boys have a longer understanding of how it works and should have known better than to make such an outrageous statement. To think that I wouldn't have given her the option is absurd. I couldn't have forced her to go. It doesn't work that way. They were stunned and shocked, both of which are understandable reactions to Grace's arbitrary illness. I just hope that the family can come together as Grace had planned for this weekend. She always put so much time into these galas. You and she both spent months organizing this. I am proud of all three of them for coming back in time." With that, he finished speaking and looked up to the somber and thick gray clouds. He closed his eyes and felt the first mist of rain begin its descent.

"I miss the children too." He chuckled. "Calling them babies may be a bit off the mark though considering the boys are approaching 24 and Patty will be 22 at years end." He laughed to himself. She gave him a sideways glance and smirked with a twinkle in her eye.

"The three of them will always be my babies, no matter what," she responded. Trish finished her breakfast and seeing that Fred had abandoned his, motioned for Reid to clear the table. Reid was in his late twenties and had been with the family for ten years. He had once had a small crush on Patty but quickly found the fascination to be one sided. He was the only employee to have had family before coming to work full time for the Skyler's. His family had worked for the Skyler's going back two generations. Grace had been his godmother. He was usually assigned to security detail for galas and when he wasn't, he spent his time as close to the Skyler's as possible by request of the couple themselves. In the capacity of a butler, hunting companion, chauffeur, and several other odds and ends jobs, he was seen as a pivotal asset to the family. Since he had been raised around the family and had worked for them part time throughout his high school and college years, he had become privy to almost all the information public and private having to do with them. Grace's death had stunned him into a seemingly unending state of depression and shock. His parents had passed away when he was in college and Grace's death the previous month had left him alone in the world. Her will bequeathed him her life savings and established his permanent place in the Skyler's employ. Following Grace's passing, Reid had been entrusted with every piece of information regarding the family and because of that was permitted to work on the residential floor as few employees were. Only the most trusted of employees worked in direct contact with the Skyler's and their children. As Reid was turning to leave the balcony, Mr. Skyler raised a question.

"How are you feeling today, Reid?" he asked. Reid exhaled and looked to Mr. Skyler.

"I am doing better every day," he said.

"Please feel free to put in with Wendy for time off. I want you to take as much time as you need," said Mrs. Skyler.

Reid smiled and thanked both for their kindness. He walked back into the house and used the employee passage just inside and along the wall leading to the balcony. He pushed the nose of the cherub sitting on the marble pedestal beside the wall and a seemingly delicate wooden panel of wall facing him slid backward and to the right revealing a stone stairwell leading to the kitchen. He walked through it and down the stairwell just in time for the panel to resume its usual place along the wall beside the statue. The Skyler's now both stood at the balcony wall overlooking the tree line.

"I understand why she made her decision, but still find myself thinking that the boys could have taken her, maybe even persuaded her to enter. She would still be with us today," he said.

"Grace wanted to be at peace. Could she have easily been saved? Yes. Asking ourselves over and over why we didn't make her go won't bring her back." Trish's voice broke on the last half and she wiped a tear from her eye. Fred exhaled and put his arm around her waist. From inside the house, the grandfather clock was heard tolling out chimes to signify that it was now seven forty-five. The couple exited the balcony to resume their daily activities. Trish and Fred walked through the drawing room and out the carved wood double doors. Fred turned to walk down the hallway toward their bedroom to dress for the day's schedule. Trish began her descent to the first floor where her office was located. Just as her foot touched the second step, she heard Fred call her name in an emotionless, yet fevered tone. She turned and walked back down the hallway to their bedroom. She was immediately struck with Fred's demeanor of stunned alarm. Fred was staring wide eyed out of the center window along the hall. His mouth hung half open and his hands hung limp at his sides.

Of the three windows on the wall, the center window provided a view of both the front of the house with its lush landscaped open yard and two iron crafted gates that permitted entry and exit to the drive leading away from the main house. The tree line extends from the front of the house to the country road three miles away where the main gate had always stood. The trees lined the route from the main cast iron gate to the two wrought iron gates that provided the first glimpse of the house. From the center window, he had a view of the house gates, but no further. Trish cautiously approached her husband along the hallway. He was staring out over the long drive. As she walked toward him, he began to speak.

"I was walking toward the room to change into my jacket when I glanced outside," he spoke very softly. She joined him at the window and immediately gasped. Her eyes became as wide as his. There, walking through the entry drive gate, along the road from the main gate, was Geoffrey.

He was visibly staring up at the center window where the couple now stood. The icy temperature outside made his breath visible as he moved with purpose toward the stone steps leading into the house. Geoffrey was dressed in his usual khaki pants, pale white shirt, and brown over jacket. His shoes were well worn and his thick brown beard had begun to turn gray along the sides. His brown curled hair was matted with sweat. In his right hand, he held a tattered, faded, and rustic dark blue sash with white floral embroidery on it. The couple exhaled after Geoffrey had reached the stone steps leading to the house. Past the sentry statues of Michael and Gabriel were seven elongated stone steps that stretched eight feet in length. Trish and Fred immediately began their hurried run to the elevator just beside the marble stairwell. The family members were the only ones permitted to use it.

The carved oak doors with the engravings 'FSP', with the 'S' being the boldest and most pronounced letter, opened and the two quickly entered. The doors closed and the antique buttons within were labeled with black bold letters instead of numbers. The large block letters began at the bottom with 'S' for security, 'P' for primary, 'G' for guests and gala and finally 'R' for residential floor. Fred quickly pressed the large black 'S' and the elevator moved rapidly. The elevator stopped and the two hurriedly approached Wendy and Richie who were standing in the lobby just outside the security main door. The walls, ceilings, and floors on the security level were made of stone and the floors had etchings of ovals carved into each stone square. The elevator doors closed and the four gathered into a tight-knit square just outside the security main door. The

Skyler's sense of alarm upon exiting the elevator was immediately evident to Wendy and Richard. Wendy had just exited the security offices and was speaking with Richie when the couple arrived, out of breath and alarmed. Wendy dropped her conversation with Richie and the two of them approached the couple.

"Where is he?" demanded Fred. Wendy was taken aback until Geoffrey came around the corner from the stairs. Still clutching the sash, he walked over to the antique wooden sofa and love seat. He motioned for the rest of the group to join him. There were no windows on the security floor. The source of lighting was from the candle wall sconces placed in six-foot increments in the stone ceiling. The appearance of the security floor itself was quite domineering in its dark and quiet nature. The five members gathered together and sat on the furniture. The rustic dark mahogany table in front of the sofa was bare. Geoffrey placed the sash lengthwise on top of the table. He bowed his head and brought his left hand to his forehead to rub his temples. His forehead was furrowed. He exhaled and sat down beside Wendy. All five were in disbelief. Trish held her hand to her sternum and sat erect. Fred blinked twice at the sash and cleared his throat. He moved his hands up and down his thighs and looked to Geoffrey for an explanation. Wendy and Richie sat open mouthed and wide-eyed staring at the sash. It had been years since that night. None of them had forgotten. This was their worst nightmare. Geoffrey stood and paced in front of the table a few times. He finally spoke.

"Lucas and Paul noticed the sash around 2:30 this morning and called me to come take a look. They saw it on the monitors. I believe that we should keep up appearances and not make assumptions. Panicking will not do us any good either," he stated. He looked to the couple and Trish stood in indignation.

"Our children are at stake here, Geoff. We ran to the elevator out of panic because—" And then she stopped. Geoff had held up his hand and Fred had risen to join his wife. He wrapped both his arms around her, and she turned to face him. He kissed her forehead and the two exhaled and retook their seats.

"I've come here to show you what was left tied to the main gate in a 'nice little bow', not to upset you Trish," he said. "I apologize for sending the two of you into a panic. While the evidence points to the obvious, I believe that it is best to keep up appearances and to continue the days schedule as originally planned. I'll work with the security team on this." He pointed to the sash. "I've requested a meeting with the two of you this evening after dinner. Now that Wendy and Richie are aware of it" – he looked to the two employees still staring at the sash – "I feel that you should be present as well." He finished speaking just as the main security door clicked open. Out of the door came Harrison. His bleach blonde hair and green eyes gave him a youthful countenance. Geoffrey crossed the room to speak with Harrison. The two of them were deep in conversation and Harrison glanced at the sash a few times in collected thought.

"Wendy, what brought you here?" asked Geoffrey. His eyebrows were furrowed. He looked to the Skyler's and they looked to Wendy and Richard. Wendy looked up from the sash for the first time and met Geoffrey's glance. She collected her thoughts and regained her composure.

"Richie came to the office this morning with the new girl, Rachel. She had walked up to the residential floor and spoke with Trish," she said. "I found it very unusual, she has been an exemplary employee this past month, and it was completely out of character for her. She would never have done that unless—" She stopped, took a deep breath, and looked down at the sash. Trish put her hand to her mouth and Fred closed his eyes and hung his head.

Richie looked to the group and stood up. He straightened his suit and said, "It seems like all indications point to his return. I hope it's not the case, but I agree with Geoff. We should carry on like nothing is wrong. I believe speaking with Rachel is in order. Harrison I'm not a fan of the bleach. Geoff, the beard is very becoming although I do miss the mustache. Trish, Rick, I believe that you'll be needing my services as will several others of the staff come December and I look forward to my new creations." He chuckled. The group laughed in unison and the tension seemed to lift from the room.

"I will see you all this evening. As always, Geoff, I put my trust in you and your security army to get to the bottom of this." He finished and walked down the hall to the portrait of the Skyler's with their sons. "I've always liked this portrait. It's a shame she wasn't there then. She would have been exquisite." He looked over the portrait of the foursome. Dressed in their finest suits, polished shoes, and ties the three men looked dignified and respectable. Mrs. Skyler was dressed in her greatest pale blue dress with her onyx and pearl necklace draped across her neck. The couple was angled toward each other with Mr. Skyler looking toward the artist and Mrs. Skyler looking fondly at her husband. The boys stood behind their parents with their backs to each other, faces toward the artist. The couple sat on a loveseat strikingly like the one in the security lobby. Richard's smile faded and his mouth drooped at the side. The night the portrait had been finished would forever be imprinted on the minds of the family. He straightened up and took a deep breath. He pushed the painting and it gave way and opened into the wall revealing a marble stairwell winding up toward the primary floor down the hall from Wendy's office. He walked through the passageway and up the stairs just as the portrait swung back into place. In the lobby, the five were discussing their next steps.

"I think Geoff's right. We should go on as usual. Until we discuss all the evidence, we can't be sure if he's here or not," Fred said. He stood kissed his wife's hand and walked toward the elevator. Trish watched him as he entered the elevator.

As soon as it had closed, she stood and said, "I want the full story tonight. Not one detail left out. If he's been seen on camera, I want to know. If the cemetery has anything missing or new, I want to know. He may have been there to leave something for Grace. I have so many things to organize that I really must go. I'll see you all this evening." She collected herself and walked toward the elevator. As she entered, Wendy approached Harrison and Geoffrey.

As the elevator rose, Wendy told Geoffrey, "If he is back, Geoff, all three of them are in danger. That night is still a vivid memory, as you well know. I want the security heightened, the whole security team assembled and put on its highest alert." Both men held Wendy in high regard, as she was the newest authority in the house since Grace's death. Wendy had spoken with Harrison about any possible changes on the grounds recently. Owing to Rachel's odd behavior, Wendy and Richie had immediately sought clarification from the assistant to the head of security, Harrison. Geoffrey, overseeing all security measures was doing his morning check-in with the ground patrols at the gates, along the cemetery and back to the stone steps leading to the rear entrance of the house. He felt that personal check-ins with security forces was more reliable than using radios and cameras. His micromanaging behavior when it came to security was cumbersome at times, but well appreciated by all. Wendy continued giving directions.

"As long as there is any doubt, I want the patrols doubled. Grace always had the security team doubled on the night of the Gala because of him. I do not see why we should change that tradition if not arrange for it to regularly occur now that he has 'possibly' made it known that he has returned. I agree with the rest of them Harry, the bleach was a poor choice," she said. Harrison opened his mouth to speak and looked to Geoffrey for support. Geoffrey merely laughed and shrugged his shoulders.

"We trust Richie to handle those matters and your experiment is a clear indication as to why," she said. "Also, the beard may be flattering but not being in the main office by 7:15 is a strong indication that your micromanaging security habit has reached an alarming level," she said with emphasis. Geoffrey raised his eyebrows and Harrison closed his mouth and took a small step back. He had seen Grace and Geoffrey exchange words in times of difficulty, but Wendy's temperament was a great deal more domineering and in Harrison's view, slightly frightening. Geoffrey began to speak but then thought better of it. He looked to Harrison and instructed him to return to the monitors and check in with the estate patrols. Harrison did as he was told. After the main door clicked shut, Geoffrey began calmly responding to Wendy's demands.

"I do not micromanage. I have a system of operation here that Grace respected and understood. The agreement between the two of us was to allow her to organize the interior decorations of inanimate objects and I would arrange all the breathing objects, for example security," he said as he waved his hand toward the main door. He looked at Wendy and she replied.

"I miss her just as much as you do Geoff. Arguing will not do us any good. I believe that the arrangement between the two of you should remain as it always was. My only request is that, with the children returning this weekend, security be heightened. Grace could not have foreseen these events, but we must be prepared to protect the family. The estate and the members herein rely on you. I'm sure you know that but for all of us, this is our family. We have to protect our family," she finished. Geoff had turned to walk back into the main office to review the security footage. He sighed and hunched his shoulders. He turned and approached Wendy.

"This is my family. Everyone here is my family. I know that everyone looks to me to maintain the safety of us all. I micromanage, yes, I admit it" – he laughed – "because I care too much for my family's well-being. I will share all knowledge of this predicament this evening. The three are returning. I didn't know that. I will plan accordingly. Like I said though, panicking will not benefit anyone. If anything, it will play right into his hands. I promise everything will be laid out in the open." He walked toward the table and picked up the sash. Wendy sighed and nodded. She thanked Geoffrey and with their conflict resolved turned to approach the family portrait. Geoff resumed his walk to the main door and entered just as the painting swung shut after Wendy.

Chapter Two

Fred's town car drove up to the front steps of the house. As he descended the steps, the driver exited the car to open the door for him. The lightning quick pace with which the driver moved gave Fred pause. He gave Teddy a stern look, but Teddy just grinned. The car turned away from the house and drove toward the manor gates.

"Teddy, it's alright to gravitate toward our God given abilities, but some of the non-residential staff could have seen you," he said passively staring out the window. As the car moved down the main drive to the primary gate, Teddy's mouth curved up at the corners.

"If anyone had seen me, it would be only too easy to convince them they're mistaken," he said glancing into the mirror toward Fred.

"Richie's given us all acting lessons and if not for him and his works of art if I do say so myself (he ran his hand through his hair with a look of narcissism) the family would have been discovered many years ago." Fred looked toward the mirror and caught Teddy's eye. Glaring at him for a few seconds, Fred sighed.

"All the same, be cautious. You never know who's watching." Teddy nodded and refocused on driving.

Turning onto the highway for the grain factory, Teddy couldn't help but wonder what could be giving Fred such deep contemplation. Fred was staring out the window when he saw the black raven flying through the trees lining the route. The bird turned its head to stare at the passenger window. Fred stared at the raven and watched as it rose in the air and flew back toward the direction of the house. Teddy noticed the raven and managed a short look into the rearview mirror to catch Fred's eye before reaching the traffic light just short of the factory.

"He's back or he's close," Teddy said matter-of-factly.

"We're not sure. I'm not jumping to any conclusions just yet." Teddy sighed in response.

"Not to state the obvious, but Walter never liked him. He knew that man was a bad seed."

"Then don't state the obvious. Geoffrey has a firm grasp on the situation and that's that."

The light turned green and the town car moved forward a half mile before turning right just after the church. Seeing how tense Teddy had become, Fred tried to alleviate his stress.

"Edgar could have put the bird out of its misery, but now she's our problem. Don't stress over a mere possibility. For one who appears to be a 'late thirties who enjoys long walks on the beach', you're well on your way to stress wrinkles, if that were possible."

"You and I both know Richie would go into a massive panic if it were," Teddy replied.

"Why are you critiquing my Craig's list ad anyway?" he asked looking into the rearview mirror.

"It's so cliché, Teddy. Go for originality."

"It wouldn't be believable if I did, not that I haven't thought about it." Teddy frowned as they reached the main entrance to the building. Four stories in height and primarily mechanical the building wasn't out of the ordinary. Having been in the town and under the ownership of the family for the town's entire history the building had been upgraded to accommodate to the growing needs of the business over time. The owner's office was on the top floor overlooking the operation. Teddy slowly approached the door and Fred left the car.

"If I told people my real age on there, I'd be getting responses from all the Lady Gagas on Craig's list," he sneered. Fred laughed and entered the building greeting each employee by first name. Teddy re-entered the car and made his way back to the estate.

In the kitchen, Rachel and several other employees stood, sat, and talked with each other while they enjoyed their breakfast. The chefs took special care that the employees as well as the family ate healthily and on a regular basis. The constant stream of activity required energy and the cooking staff knew that all too well. As a result, the kitchen staff, who were all veterans, required employees to eat in the extensive kitchen at the start and finish of each of their respective shifts. Maggie and Steven were the head chefs for the household for as long as anyone could remember. Maggie stood at five foot seven with flats and Steven stood at six foot one. Maggie was kneading dough with her hands at the oak table set against the north wall. She was preparing a ravioli dinner for the family while the rest ate their breakfast. The walls of the kitchen were completely made of stone, as were the floors. The kitchen staff could choose the décor of this one area over a century ago and they chose the same as the security team had. Security staff would stop by most of the day unannounced and pick at whatever food was lying around with Maggie slapping their hands whenever she caught them on something. Steven was grilling up some pancakes and eggs at the stove adjacent to the kitchen door. The windows in the kitchen were placed along the north wall evenly spaced apart just below the ceiling. The room was one of the largest in the house owing to necessity. The kitchen held one magnificent stove with twelve burners, two wall-mounted ovens that each held up to three wonderful turkeys (tried and true every thanksgiving), three triple sized refrigerators for gala dinners, family gatherings, and general food storage. From the windows in the north wall, the thick grey clouds overtaking the sky could be seen. As with the security floor, the kitchen had candle wall sconces along the walls evenly spaced apart. The kitchen was placed on the first floor just three doors down from the planning office and Wendy was known to pop in unannounced to see if anyone was loitering in the kitchen. The morning staff was seated and standing around the elongated red oak table in the center of the room just in front of the kitchen door. Reid appeared from behind a portrait of an anonymous young man standing in front of a black lake encircled with white frost. The portrait swung inward and Reid stepped through into the kitchen. Conversation temporarily halted as Reid approached the sink in the far corner to deliver the breakfast discarded by the Skyler's. Maggie's back was facing the breakfast table and she heard the lull in conversation and turned to face the group as Reid neared the sink.

"Well, I assume since the talking is finally done that you are all finished with breakfast. Turn in your plates then and either go home, if your done for the day or continue with your shift," she said with no emotion. The staff simply stared at her and Reid took his place at the table once another employee had vacated the seat after Maggie's speech. No one else said a word and Steven could tell the employees were frozen in place. He emptied the pancake pan onto the plate in the center of the table. He placed the final pancake on top of the center stack. He cleared his throat and caught the table's attention.

"For those of you not finished this morning, please continue," he calmly stated. Maggie took a great breath in and exhaled shaking her head and turned to resume her kneading. Steven finished making the last of the bacon and placed it on the table as well. Reid was helping himself to some pancakes when the conversation restarted.

"What were you thinking? Talking to Mrs. Skyler out of the blue like that. That is career suicide. In times like these being fed by some of the best chefs, earning a steady income, knowing that maybe someday I could be a 'residential' (Jackie whispered), living in this house…" She shook her head. "I would not chance that for anything," she finished. Jackie had been a 'non' for about five years and only once had she seen the Skyler's as a whole family. She kept to herself but listened closely to the gossip around town trying to get to the bottom of the mystery behind the family. The family kept to itself, sure enough, but the five had something different about them that the town simply couldn't place.

"I don't know what came over me," Rachel began. "I just suddenly found myself walking up the stairs and talking to Mrs. Skyler. Thank God that Richie came along because I have no idea what I was saying to her. It felt like I was saying someone else's words. I can't describe it exactly, but it felt robotic," she finished. The staff was all ears during her speech and open-mouthed. Reid, Maggie, and Steven stopped what they were doing and turned to stare at her. Rachel sipped her orange juice and began eating her second pancake. Jackie and the others continued eating and wondered what to make of her speech.

"What did the 'rez' floor look like?" Jordan asked. Jackie looked at him in disbelief.

"She wanders up to the 'rez' floor and speaks directly to the queen bee and that's your only question. No wonder you're still working the dawn patrol." She huffed. Jordan had been assigned to patrol the house gates and the tree line with the rest of the 'nons' in the security department. He had been working the same shift for two years. From midnight until daybreak, he and half a dozen other 'nons' would patrol the house gates, walk along the tree line parallel to them and back to the gates ensuring nothing had been changed and no one had trespassed past the main gate three miles away. Having 'nons' learn how to patrol the property was Geoff's way of bringing in new talent to protect the estate and the family within. Using grueling work schedules and periodic emergency drills, the new security employees learned how to expect anything and to defend the estate accordingly. Training the 'nons' to protect the estate and providing them with food and shelter each morning, gave them pride for the house and in the end all of the permanent security wound up living inside its walls. Jackie was not privy to that information, so Jordan merely sneered at her over his eggs. Reid resumed his breakfast and the chefs returned to their morning work.

"Richie called my name, and, in my confusion, I began apologizing for being there, but I also took a look around as we left to come down here," she said with a low voice. All the 'nons' were leaning in to listen to her now. She continued speaking at a low volume and the staff was attuned to every word. Reid sipped his orange juice and paid close attention to her speech. He silently acknowledged the sideways glances from Maggie and Steven whose blank stares at their respective workstations would soon attract attention if not reassured by him. Reid had moved into the house over the summer and only the long-term staff knew of it.

"The boy's look gorgeous in the pictures on that floor. The family photos are so candid and relaxed. The atmosphere up there is completely different from what is portrayed to the rest of us. The pictures up there of Mr. and Mrs. Skyler with the boys look fairly old," she said while furrowing her eyebrows. Reid snorted.

"That's it." He laughed. "You saw an old photo, some family photos, and that's worthy of gossiping over," he said. The rest of the table looked at him with some of them squinting their eyes at him. Maggie and Steven smiled from their respective occupations. Jackie and Rachel resumed their conversation choosing to ignore Reid. Jackie began questioning Rachel.

"What do you mean they were gorgeous? Do the pictures look different up there as opposed to the other floors?" she asked. Rachel shook her head and swallowed another piece of breakfast.

"The photos are sepia. The clothes they wear are from another time. The family photos up there are definitely of them, but the way they style their hair, Mr. and Mrs. Skyler too, they all four look different. The most interesting part was the painting above the fireplace in the drawing room," she said. She stopped to pick more pieces of bacon from the pile on to her plate. Reid was staring at her with his fork hovering above his plate and the rest of the staff including Maggie and Steven had turned to look at her. Maggie's look of concern turned to one of amusement as she thought of something. Steven caught her eye and Maggie nodded. The two of them returned to their work and Steven began to laugh. The staring crowd along the table looked to Steven. Still laughing he half turned and acknowledged his audience.

"Mrs. Skyler took a photography class a few years ago. For fun one summer, she had the family pick out some antique clothes and even had some of us residential staff join in on the fun. She took the pictures and placed them throughout the house. Not just on the residential floor but throughout the estate you'll find them." He smiled. The staff looked at him and any lingering curiosity vanished, and Rachel was left just as confused as she had been when she entered the kitchen. Jordan still had a question to ask of Rachel.

"What about Patty?" he asked with raised eyebrows. "What did she look like?" Several other male members of the staff were waiting anxiously for her response. Anyone paying attention to Maggie and Steven would have noticed the sudden freeze and intake of breath. Reid too was frozen in place as he had forgotten, albeit briefly about Patty. Rachel cleared her throat. Wiping her mouth with her napkin, she brought her eyebrows together.

"I don't remember seeing her in the pictures," she said. The staff looked at her with suspicion. They looked at each other around the table and those standing looked equally as suspicious.

"What do you mean you didn't see her?" Jackie asked. "How could you possibly miss Helen of Troy? Even in a sepia photo, you'd be able to spot her before either of those two magnificent men," she spoke the last words with the hint of a moan. She had always spent her mornings crooning over the eyes and faces of the Skyler twins. The men at the table groaned and the women sighed. Maggie and Steven had heard enough. Reid rose to leave the kitchen but before he did, he approached Maggie.

"Maggie," he stated. She turned to him and gave him a look of concern. The rest of the employees were finishing up their breakfast and resumed their conversations.

"The Skyler's were talking this morning about the twins and Patty coming home for the gala," he said. Maggie and Steven looked to each other. The staff continued to talk about the party they were planning this weekend at one of the clubs in town. The issue of the Skyler children returning brought conversation to a low murmur with ears perked with attention to the conversation between Reid and Maggie. Maggie peered around Reid and raised her eyebrows at the seated and standing members of the staff. Most of the employees had finished their breakfasts and were simply talking about their plans for the upcoming weekend. Some of the staff had been staring at Reid and Maggie while Steven continued to prepare the afternoon's lunch for the staff and family. The kitchen door swung open to reveal Wendy. She looked very calm and yet unsurprised to find most of the morning staff sitting and standing around the elongated red oak table. She looked at each employee in the eye one at a time. The conversation came to a complete stop and the only sound was the kitchen staff shifting pans and adding spices to their respective works. The seated staff rose from the table some wiping their mouths with their napkins while the standing slowly placed their plates on the table and wiped crumbs from their uniforms.

"I see that you have been taking your time this morning. How were the pancakes?" she asked the group. Murmurs of affirmation were followed by a nod from Wendy. "Don't let me keep you from your work. I wouldn't want any of you to fall behind in the day's schedule," she said. The employees began leaving but just as the first employee was exiting the kitchen door she added, "by the way, it would behoove you all to check the planning room. Adjustments have been made to everyone's schedule to prepare for the gala this weekend."

She smiled at each employee and they made a false grin in return as they left. In truth, she had been listening at the door and the upcoming gala would destroy any plans of a night out that they were all hoping to enjoy. Maggie and Steven turned from their respective chores and greeted Wendy with a smile. Reid was still standing by Maggie. Wendy approached Reid and hugged him. He was still having difficulty coping with the loss of his godmother and at times spent all day in the kitchen to be close to Maggie and Steven who had helped him to cope after his parent's death.

"Morning, Reid." She smiled. She turned and said the same to Maggie and Steven. "Richie tells me that the twins and Patty are coming back for the gala," she said.

"Reid was just telling me the same thing. I think it's good that they're coming back. I'm sure Trish is thrilled," Maggie replied. She moved the pans of ravioli to the freezer. Steven was frying up some chicken on the stove.

"It's about time they came back. The funeral was hard on all of us, but to fight openly like that. We have to keep up appearances and I thought for sure they would ruin it with their screaming at each other all the time. It's not like the staff wasn't listening. At least, we're lucky enough to know that it would sound insane to an outsider, but obviously someone, someday will put it together and then what?" He shook his head and moved the pan to another burner and began testing a few of the sauces that were on the other burners. Wendy stood by Reid and asked Maggie how long dinner was expected to be tonight. Maggie regularly planned her meals by how long each would take to be eaten. Years ago, she would time each course while the family was at dinner and serve accordingly. Owing to her length of service with the family, she now had a system of operation in the kitchen that was only rivaled by Grace's 'Skyler System'. Steven's attention shifted back to his work when an employee drew his gaze to a poorly made sauce. Maggie leaned against the wood table and addressed Wendy.

"If the trio comes back, I'm confident that Geoffrey will be on high alert. Not to mention all the new security installments since the last time. It's been…well, a long time," she said as she stared off toward the portrait on the wall. Reid followed her gaze.

"I think I'm going to see if Fred and Trish need me for anything else today," Reid said. With that, he left the kitchen and made his way to the third floor via the portrait on the kitchen wall.

"I have the utmost confidence in Geoff. I also have a profound understanding of what *he's* capable of," Wendy spoke softly. Maggie nodded and restated her support for Geoff and his security army. Steven called Maggie's attention to the oven where chicken breasts were about to meet their blackened end. With that, the conversation ended and the kitchen resumed its hyperactive pace. Wendy took her leave of the kitchen and resumed her daily tour of the estate in the hopes of catching one of the 'nons' behaving lackadaisically.

Richie stood in line for the planning room as the employees queued to see their respective schedule changes. In the middle of complaints being muttered under their breaths, Richie found his way behind Rachel. Several staff had removed their phones from their pockets to text friends that tonight's party was being called off. It was left to Jordan to call the club itself to cancel all the entertainment planned for the evening. The dour faces were beginning to annoy Richie and he decided to strike up conversation with Rachel. Knowing how the staff enjoyed it when veterans voluntarily spoke to 'nons' he took the opportunity to lighten the mood.

"How are you doing, Rachel?" he asked as several employees curbed their complaints. Those who had picked up their schedule changes hovered around the corners hoping to catch the conversation. Wendy's appearance and lingering stare toward the planning room jostle from the entryway to the kitchen caused an immediate dispersal of staff that had picked up their changes.

"Those of you who have completed your shifts should try and enjoy what's left of the" – she looked to her watch and saw that it was approaching eight thirty – "morning," she said with a smile. The staff falsely grinned in return and expedited their schedule retrieval and departure. Those still in the queue had their ears perked for the conversation between Richie and Rachel. Wendy departed the corridor to survey the rest of the floors.

"I don't know why I walked up to the residential floor. Am I going to lose my job?" she asked weakly. The staff's other conversation had died down to a low murmur and some had made soft intakes of breath waiting for Richard's response.

Richie laughed. "No, of course not. It's the first time you have ever done anything out of the ordinary. I must ask you though, what made you decide to speak to Mrs. Skyler this morning? Did you have upcoming plans that necessitated an immediate change? You see I am trying to understand what provoked such a random act from you," he finished. Exhaling could be heard throughout the hall and in the office. Rachel was one of the favorites among the 'nons'. She was quite beautiful in an understated manner. She had been offered dinner by several of the men within the estate and always politely turned them down. She was always exceedingly polite and cared for her fellow employees when they were sick or upset about something.

Having only worked for the estate a month, she was gaining the reputation of being quite maternal when it came to the employees. After Grace's death, she seemed to calm Reid and whenever an employee was sick or feeling less than motivated to do their daily work she was there with words of inspiration and compassion.

"Well truth be told, I've met someone. He seems to be very kind and has been understanding of my work schedule. However, our dinner dates tend to run well past midnight and I have had difficulty maintaining my usual work pace because of it," she said. The men in the queue looked down to their feet and several of the women were anxious to ask her later whom the man was. Gossip about anything while working made coming to the estate that much more intriguing.

"I see. Perhaps your boyfriend could cut the hours back just a little so that you could come to work feeling less exhausted," Richie suggested. Rachel's cheeks began to turn a slight shade of pink.

"It's not that formal yet. We just enjoy talking. We have dinner sometimes but on the whole, we spend the night walking around and just…talking about everything and anything," she said. Jackie was in front of Rachel and Jordan stood just inside the door of the planning office.

"Does he know where you work? Perhaps if he understood the time constraints you were under." He stopped as Rachel interrupted.

"Oh he knows where I work. He was actually really interested in my job," she said with a beaming smile, "how many guys can I meet that are excited to hear about vacuuming and dusting in a mansion." She chuckled. Jackie had every intention of questioning Rachel during lunch. Her curiosity was continually piqued with the conversation. Jordan and Jackie picked up their schedules and left the room. Jackie exchanged a long glance with Rachel to let her know they were definitely going to be talking about the guy later on. Rachel smiled and continued talking with Richie. The two of them picked up their work schedules and departed the room. All eyes were on the duo as they walked down the hall for the main lobby of the house. Richie was beginning to grow concerned about the man.

"You said he was interested in your job?" Richie raised his eyebrows slightly. Rachel nodded.

"He asks me questions about it. For example, the other night he asked me how long I had worked for the estate. I told him. Then he asked if I really enjoyed waking up so early to merely clean a few rooms, his words not mine," she said as Richards's eyes became more focused on her expressions.

"Is that why you wanted to change your schedule?" he asked.

"Well, I wasn't overly sure that I wanted to change my schedule because I don't know how cumbersome it would be to rearrange for Wendy. I was concerned that I may not be scheduled as much if I asked for a change this early in my working here," she explained. Richie simply stared at her.

"Drew suggested that I speak to Mrs. Skyler directly about my schedule so as not to over burden Wendy. I told him that's not the protocol for schedule changes and he said that it would surely help me to excel in my career if Mrs. Skyler could identify me from the 'working drones in the

Skyler hive'," she said using air quotes with her fingers. Richard's face took on a serious disposition. Rachel wasn't sure what she had said so she simply looked at Richard.

"You say his name is Drew," Richie stated very slowly. Rachel nodded unsure of where the serious tone had come from. Rachel swallowed and Richie continued his query.

"Is that short for something?"

"Andrew." Rachel felt as if she was glued to the spot. Richie relaxed his composure enough to put Rachel at ease.

"He is very eloquent and well mannered. He mentioned that he had taken Jackie out for dinner a few times but found the conversation to be slightly banal. Again, his words. He talks as if he were from somewhere else. I asked him where he's from." Rachel had slowed in her elaboration of events because Richie had tensed again.

"Where did he say he was from?"

"He said a little bit of everywhere," she responded with no emotion. Richie had heard enough. Rachel had about two and a half hours left in her working day before she was finished. Richie regained his normal composure.

"I think he sounds like a decent young man but don't let him get in the way of work. Sadly, there have been too many instances of female employees working here that find dating and working to be a distraction. Several of them have quit as a result or have had their romances ended due to the demands of the job. I would hate for you to lose your job or have your emotions toyed with all because a man is eloquent and well mannered," he explained. "I have to continue my shift as do you I believe, but I hope your relationship turns out better than most," he finished. The warnings Richie had given left her wondering how demanding a house worker job could be. He left her in the lobby and walked up the marble stairwell to resume his duties on the third floor. Jackie was standing adjacent to the coatroom located just beside the main entry door to the house. It was situated behind a rather imposing antiquated oak door depressed into the wall. The room was for employees to use just as they entered so that they could check in and get straight to work in an efficient manner instead of mulling around and wasting time placing their coats in disarray or wearing them for the duration of their shift. Jordan stood on the steps just outside the soaring oak doors that permitted entrance to the house. He had his hands in the pockets of coat. Jackie looked to Jordan whose head was cocked to the side now and the two of them smirked at each other. Jordan had broad shoulders and was equally as powerfully built as Reid. Jackie had patiently waited for Richie to disappear up the stairs. Following his departure, she approached Rachel while Jordan's gaze followed very closely. Jackie had her leather bag slung over her shoulder. The freezing temperatures from outside didn't seem to faze her. Her hair had attracted some static and a few fly aways were standing erect on her head. While this sight amused Rachel, she was still confused about the day's events. The Skyler's employee charter bus pulled up to the front steps as Jackie began talking to Rachel. Jordan turned to face the bus and descended the house steps to board it.

"Are you okay?" she asked. Seeing Rachel speak to Richie was strange but watching their facial expressions during their conversation had alarmed Jackie. Rachel sighed and slightly hung her head.

"He said I'm not fired. That's a relief." She laughed nervously. "I don't know why, but I started telling him about the man I was texting you about. The longer he looked me in the eye the more I told him." She looked over Jackie's shoulder and saw Jordan standing in the doorway to the bus, staring at the two of them. She looked back to Jackie.

"Well if he said you're still working that's definitely a good sign. Getting you to spill all about your personal life without really even trying is" – she squinted her eyes and stared at the floor – "disturbing," she finished. Jackie told Rachel she would talk to her later today.

"Text me when you're leaving, and I'll meet you at The Grill," she said as she turned to exit the front doors. Ascending the steps to the bus, she looked up at Jordan. He took his seat inside and as the door to the bus shut, Rachel re-ascended the marble stairwell to complete her work for the morning.

The employee bus shuttled the non-residential staff to and from work every day. The idea had developed years earlier in order to better accommodate the non-residential staff. While the estate does regularly bus in tourists who pay to visit the property, the estate has no parking for employees, residential, or not. This countered with the remote location of the property made it necessary to shuttle the non-residential staff from their respective apartments to the estate three times a day. The shuttle itself had been modified inside to accommodate the needs of the staff. The television screens were attuned to weather, the daily assignments drawn up by Wendy as well as the available breakfast and lunch options created by Steven and Maggie. Each seat was assigned to specific staff for their specific arrival and departure time from and to the estate. To this end, the pouches on the back of each seat contained odds and ends of specific chores to be done that day whether it was a security personnel being reminded to create their gym membership required by all security employees or the newest employee being given a range of gated apartment brochures to peruse over that gave significant discounts to Skyler employees. Each employee placed their thumbs on the center console just after climbing the stairs into the bus. The bus monitored what time each employee sat down and the procedure was repeated upon exiting the shuttle. As the bus drove through the house gate down the main drive, several employees were closing their eyes and relaxing for the first time. Several of the security personnel had been at the estate since four thirty that morning and the shuttle ride back to their apartments was a welcome respite. The drive was nearly thirty-five minutes, and, in that time, some talked while others slept. As the bus passed through the main gate and turned onto the highway a security guard waved to the driver and he waved back. As the trees whipped past the shuttle along the road, Jordan and Jackie looked back to catch a final glimpse of the estate. Though the manor could not be seen from the road, the iron gate that closed behind them leant a sense of finality to their working day. Jackie sighed and leaned back into her chair. She closed her eyes and Jordan laughed at her.

Eyes still closed, she mumbled, "What?" Jordan shrugged and leaned back in his own chair. His eye was caught by the papers in the pouch of the chair in front of him. He sat up and pulled the light-yellow parchment from its place. He was being assigned to extra hours on the night of the gala. His schedule in the planning room had said he was off duty that night owing to his inexperience when it came to interior security. Having worked there for two years, he spent the largest portion of his time learning to patrol the property for unforeseen intruders. He had wondered what criminal in their right mind would travel this far away from the city just to stumble through an almost impenetrable forest only to be stopped by two different sets of iron gates and an army for a security team. He was very confused by the note and the number on the bottom was Geoffrey's cell phone. The instructions read: *Change of plan. Call for specific directions as soon as you get home.* He sighed and placed the paper back in the pouch. He leaned back in his chair and stared up at the screen. Jackie had felt him move in his chair. She opened her eyes and turned her head to look at Jordan.

"What's up?"

"I'm not sure. Just some changes in my scheduling."

"Can we get a refund from the club?" Jackie asked as she turned to look out the window. Jordan refocused his attention on their conversation.

"I'm sure we can. It's not as if we can't find another day and another opportunity. The town loves it when the Skyler non's run amuck. It lets them know some of us are normal." He grinned. Jackie smiled while still gazing out the window. She was still thinking about Rachel and Richard's conversation and the way Richie had reacted toward her. It wasn't like him to strike up a conversation with a non. In her years as an employee, Richie had never said more than a 'good morning' to her.

"I told Rachel to text me when she clocks out. I'm interested to know why Richie would be so attentive to a random act."

"You're reading into things again."

"Something's up. Has he ever talked to you? Can you name one time when any residential employee has voluntarily struck up a conversation with you?" She turned her head to look at him. He was staring at the ceiling. He tilted his head to glance at her and then returned it to center. He shook his head.

"Something's up." Jordan peered around at the other security nons on the bus and saw that they too had yellow parchments. He squinted his eyes and lay back in his chair. All of the security guards were being called in. He took a deep breath and exhaled subtly enough while closing his eyes. His goal was to make Jackie realize that nothing was wrong. He opened one eye and glanced over to Jackie. She had turned her head to the window again and was lost in thought. The rest of the drive back to the specified apartments for the employees was silent between the two. The remainder of the bus was either softly chattering away or sleeping. The bus slowly approached the outskirts of town. As it stopped at a traffic light, the people in town could be seen giving the tinted windowed charter bus a cursory once over. People moved in and out of the gas station juxtaposed to the light with some glancing at the Skyler bus while others seemed not to care about it at all. The light turned green and as the bus slowly lurched forward and was just entering the intersection, a green Ducati with an intent rider cut across the intersection leading to the camping grounds where some of the local college population liked to spend their weekends. The driver of the bus stomped on the brakes causing the occupants within to vault forward in their seats. Some of the employees that had been sleeping looked around at the rest of their peers for an explanation. Some of the security team stood and watched the motorcycle ride down the street toward the campground.

"Plate," Jordan demanded.

"ABJ 364. California?" a security peer responded. Jordan brought his eyebrows together. The driver had started the buses forward movement again and told the employees to retake their seats.

"Just got a text from the guys at Riverview. They said they reserved the meeting room for us. What's going on Jordan?" Cam asked him. Cam started working for the Skyler's a year after Jordan was hired. He was seated beside Jordan and Jackie across the aisle on the bus. He had stood just as several others in the bus had and watched the Ducati speed away. The bus was a regular occurrence in town and most motorists in town obeyed the traffic laws. Logically speaking, an outsider would be expected to run the light so a California plate came as no surprise. The plate number was relayed back to their co-workers at the apartment complex. Combined with the day's odd events, the meeting at Riverview was going to be eventful. They passed the local cemetery as they drew nearer to the center of town. The church beside it had been the first church constructed when the town was created. Its design was typical of the nineteenth century. Having survived the weather, economic depressions, and social changes for the past two centuries the church was in remarkable condition. The stone architecture on the building had been chipped away in places but on the whole the church could not be called antiquated or grand. It stood as one rectangular shape with a single bell tower at its entryway. The churches stone exterior made the building looked aged. Its steeple was topped with a simple, yet dignified brass cross. The building was set on a hill with grass mounds arching away from it on either side. There were three stone steps leading up to the narthex's aged wood doors. The parking lot adjacent to the church wasn't large and remained vacant until Sunday mornings. The church held about five hundred people and owing to its natural proximity, the Skyler's and their employees attended each Sunday if they were not previously affiliated with another denomination. The church was considered a historical landmark but was in constant use every Sunday by the Skyler's as well as the town's population for worship services, weddings and the like.

The bus turned onto Fowler Street for the Riverview apartment complex. As it pulled through the gates of Riverview, the security guard sitting in the booth gave the driver a wave. The security booth permitted entry to Riverview each day and night by individually checking each driver, confiscating their driver's license, and asking them who they were visiting and upon their exit would return their identification to them. The complex was one of the most secure in the area. The Skyler bus was a regular sight to the residents of Riverview. There were several people within the complex that worked for the hospital, schools, banks, and the like. Those who didn't work for the estate didn't give the bus notice. Having seen the bus and its occupants thrice daily the wonder of the controlled Skyler bus system had worn off. Seeing the employees disembark the bus looking exhausted and worn from their varying shifts created speculation, but no one approached or inquired about their jobs.

While Jackie and the rest of the employees exited the bus and made beelines for their respective apartments, the security team approached the main office where the night and afternoon security team were waiting in the meeting room. Once assembled the room became very quiet. Jordan sat in one of the chairs along the side of the long oak table. Several others sat while more stood around the table and in the corners of the room. There were yawns, cracking of knuckles, necks, and such. In the middle of the table sat a black triangular speakerphone.

All assembled, the security team dialed Geoffrey's cell phone. After two rings, he picked up.

"Morning guys," he said.

"Morning," was the intermittent reply from the room.

"I need everyone in tonight at 11:30, sharp. If you're early, you're on time. If you're on time, you're late and if you're late, don't bother showing up." After his speech, the only sound on the phone was the dial tone. Still baffled, the boys dialed their connection at the sheriff's office. He picked up on the first ring.

"Guys, I plugged in the plate and got nothing." Sighs, groans, and mutters of aggravation flowed through the room. After the long and confusing day, this plate request was supposed to be a walk in the park.

"What do you mean nothing!" screamed one.

"Did you do it right?" questioned another.

"What about stolen vehicles?" Jordan asked above the rest. The room fell to a quiet murmur.

"Guys this is not my first time," the voice stated. "I did look at stolen vehicles. The bike went missing from a California dealership a little over a month ago."

"A dealership?" was the puzzled response from the group.

"Yeah. Apparently, the man arrived with a helmet and jacket on. Walked in, took the keys, and sped off. The manager was livid according to the report. The bike had no plate at the time, which is why I couldn't find anything. Although I do appreciate the complete lack of faith in my considerable skills in this area," he finished. The room was full of huffs, hung heads, and belated apologies.

"Thanks for the info," Jordan added.

"You're welcome. By the way, what time does the party start tonight?" he asked. Groans, sighs, and a series of men shaking their heads were followed by Jordan's statement, "It's been cancelled. Thanks for the help." Jordan hung up the speaker and leaned back in his chair.

"Okay. So, we're all meeting at 11:30 tonight. The gala is two days from now. No club time. Did I leave anything out?" A few of the first years in the room threw out some suggestions.

"All day today is open, until 11:30, so…" said one.

"We could have a makeshift pool party, grill up some steaks, burgers. Have some beer, a few kegs," another recommended. Jordan stared at the speakerphone.

Another employee chimed in with a statement of finality that the newer employees hadn't fully considered.

"Coupled with the gym workouts that everyone in this room participates in, the likelihood of all of us getting back in time for an apartment party to get hammered only to face Geoffrey a few hours later doesn't seem like the best idea. I do appreciate the stalwart effort to keep the party alive though. Oh and the fact that it's going to be in the low twenties tonight so no one will be touching the pools or the volleyball courts" – he looked around to the two who had made the suggestions while some of the men grinned – "just might dampen the prospect of any kind of outside festivities," he finished. Jordan and a few of the others laughed.

"Alright, well, that settles things," Jordan said. The room emptied out and the team headed toward their respective apartments. Shortly after changing out of their work clothes the roar of mustang engines, pick-ups and SUVs could be heard throughout the complex. As the men made their way to the town gym fifteen minutes from the apartment, work was in full swing at the estate.

Chapter Three

Rachel entered the first drawing room on the second floor. The room was antiquated much like the rest of the house, but grand in scale in order to accommodate a wide array of guests. The fireplace in the east wall was breathtaking in its grandeur and yet a warm relief to the increasingly cold temperatures outside. In two days' time, the drawing room would play host to an assortment of the guests directed there prior to the gala. Power duster in hand she approached the lamp tables, coffee table and mantle with precision. Just over the mantle hung a painting of the Skyler family from the mid-nineteenth century. As she perused the mantle with the power duster, the portrait caught her eye. Looking up at it, she noticed the differences in this painting and the one on the residential floor from this morning. The figures depicted in the painting were the ancestors of the present family.

While a close resemblance to the family members wouldn't necessitate a second look at the painting, a mirror image to a family member in the space of two hundred years is something that raises questions. The painting on the residential floor had the initial Skyler family consisting of Mr. and Mrs. Skyler and their three sons. The portrait over the mantle portrayed almost the same portrait but without the third son. The resemblance of the four to the present Skyler's was uncanny. While she was staring into the eyes of the figures, she felt a slight vibration in her pocket. She blinked twice, temporarily distracted from her observation, and rested her hand against the pocket. The window cleaner outside the room, perched on scaffolding, noticed her lost in thought and tapped on the glass. She approached the window with a grin. Through the glass, she could see him laughing. Another veteran, he had been cleaning the outside of the windows for several years, as he was one of the few not afraid of heights on the staff. She unlocked the window and pushed it out toward the man.

"Good morning," she said with a smile. He smiled back and perched his hands on the windowsill.

"I see you've begun admiring the past generations?" He grinned. She felt her cheeks turn hot and dropped her gaze to the floor. "Just be careful you're not caught staring at the portraits by anyone else. People might think you're obsessed like that other girl, what's her name?" He looked up lost in thought and scratched his head. "Julie, Jade, Jenny," he rambled off the names that came first to his head.

"Jackie," she said matter-of-factly. He nodded.

"Yeah, that one." She nodded and he pulled the window toward him and pushed it toward Rachel. With one last smile between them, she locked the window shut and the two went about their daily chores. As she left the room to retrieve the vacuum, the window cleaner took the rag off the window and put on a more serious demeanor. Looking into the room at the painting and back the way Rachel had left, he knew she wasn't looking on in any adoring way but in a more speculative manner. She knew something or thought she did. He moved up to the third floor set of windows as Rachel returned to the room. Lost in thought she began cleaning the carpet. Sashaying the vacuum forward and back, recalling the day's events so far. The whirr of the machine pushed her further into contemplation. *The pictures on the residential floor had included residential staff in period costumes*, she thought to herself. Apart from those that currently worked for the family, she didn't recognize most of them. Staring at the carpet without seeing it her eyebrows drew together as she pieced the information together. If the sepia photos were distributed throughout the house, then why did the photos on the residential floor only consist of the initial Skyler family from the mid-nineteenth century? There weren't any color photos on this floor either. Apart from the painting over the fireplace, the main room and the subjects of the photographs seemed little changed from its initial occupants. The odds of the family in the painting being the same as the current family, was laughable. She shook her head and smiled.

Having finished with the first drawing room, she shifted her focus to the remaining chores of the day. Walking out into the hall, she heard the first group of tourists coming through the front door downstairs. Muffled conversations along with the voices of infants here and there while the guide gently but loudly reminded them that flash photography was prohibited inside the house. She was leaning over the stairwell to catch a glimpse of the tourists. She smirked as she saw the awe light up in their eyes as they took in the intricacies of the house. Some of the tourists had headsets over their ears listening to a pre-recorded version of the guided tour. The hairs on the back of her neck stood up as she realized there was someone behind her.

"If there's time for leaning, there's time for cleaning," Richie stated. She knew she had just enough time to finish the other two rooms on the second floor before the tour moved upstairs. The window cleaner had finished up his day and the people that cleaned the stairs had finished hours ago and wouldn't interrupt the tour. She turned and nodded. A short while later she finished her work and descended the stairs for the coat closet in the foyer. She slipped her hand in her pocket revealing a missed text from Drew. Smiling ever so slightly, she put it back, retrieved her coat, and set off through the front doors for the waiting bus and a group of morning staff. Some yawned while others had partaken of more than five cups of coffee and were sufficiently wired for the day and talkative as a result. They boarded the bus for Riverview and for the first time since four that morning they could relax, mingle, or just stare off into space. The bus ride back to the apartments was for some of the staff the most peaceful time of their day. As per most of the staff, cell phones were taken out and calls made, texts typed and while the music overhead brought a lull over the bus Rachel stared out the window lost in thought.

Arriving at Riverview with its man-made pond in the middle and wooden signs hammered into the grass reading 'do not bathe in water', brought smiles to everyone on board. Deep sighs of relaxation were heard throughout the bus. While disembarking, children could be seen running along the edge of the pond in swimsuits. Their parents ran after them to no avail as the children shrieked with laughter and ran as fast as their short legs could carry them. Rachel watched them running and laughed at the parents following. A little brown-haired girl managed to get her ankles in the water just before her mother scooped her up in her arms. The littlest of giggles followed by a kiss on the forehead from her mother and a look that told her not to do that again ended the children's play.

She climbed the stairs to her and Jackie's apartment on the second floor. Opening the door, she was greeted by the aroma from the wall plug-ins and smiled. Sixty days on and they still worked. Jackie was allergic to all things floral, so Rachel had bought scented wall plug ins to spice up the place a bit. For the first time all day, she looked through her texts and read the one from Drew: another invitation to dinner. After talking with Richie today, she thought a few days apart from Drew would be good for the both of them and texted an excuse. She took a shower and changed into some jeans and a plaid three quarter length shirt. Her habit had always been to grab whatever was on top of the pile and wear it even if she'd worn in three times that week, she didn't care. She didn't pay attention to her clothes and never really bothered with anything that required her to put forward effort when not working. To that end, make-up was her archenemy and she preferred to simply wear lip gloss much to the dismay of Jackie who absolutely adored make up parties and once asked Rachel to attend one with her. She pulled her hair back into a tangled mess and left to meet Jackie at the Grill. The restaurant was a local favorite due to its wall TVs updating people about the latest sports coverage and offered the run of the mill food options along with nightly performances from whatever band they had managed to schedule for the evening. She started her car, and the beat-up little coupe flashed a maintenance light at her with the message 'engine will start soon'. Rachel sighed and said, "Okay, I'll wait." No sooner had she said it than the engine turned over and she was able to leave the complex to meet Jackie.

Ten minutes later, she arrived and saw through the window that Jackie was sitting in a booth with a milkshake already set before her. In a state of admiration, Rachel sat down. Jackie had managed to get the milkshake before her food. With the grill being notorious for giving its customers their preordered milkshakes as they gave them the check, this was really something of a feat. Rachel stared at the glass and up at Jackie in mock surprise. Jackie laughed and told her she found the secret to getting a shake at the Grill.

"I looked the guy dead in the eye and spoke slowly but with determination. He couldn't look away," she said in such a serious tone that one would think she was giving away national secrets. Rachel smirked and nodded.

"I told him that if he didn't give me my shake before my lunch I would go to his manager and tell him what a terrible waiter he was and ensure that he would never work here again."

"Mhm. What'd you really say to him?"

"I told him to please, please, please give me my shake first. He said okay and laughed." She shrugged. The boy returned and took Rachel's request for chicken strips and fries. No sooner had he gone than Jackie began prodding her with questions about her friend. Rachel felt a little bit like a traitor having known that Jackie had been on a few dates with him. She slowly revealed who it was, and Jackie was more wary than injured by the confession. Seeing her cautious glance, Rachel brought her eyebrows together.

"I'm sorry, Jackie. I know I should have brought it up before, but I didn't want to hurt you." Rachel sighed with relief. She had been keeping the secret of her dinner dates for quite some time and felt the burden of it come off her shoulders the minute she told Jackie.

"I'm not hurt by your dates with him. Did he tell you to keep it a secret?"

"He said he didn't want to come between us." Jackie's eyes flashed with anger.

The boy returned with their food and could see a serious discussion was taking place.

"Did he tell you that he broke it off with me? Rachel, Drew can be very manipulative." She emphasized the last words. "The minute he started questions about the family, I knew something wasn't right about him." Rachel looked puzzled.

"Most people are curious about them, aren't they? I mean what did he want to know that put you on guard?"

"Everything. Anything. He kept asking about the twins and where they were. He wanted to know the daily schedules of Mr. and Mrs. Skyler and how I came to work there. At first, it was sweet for him to take an interest in such a boring job as ours are," she said as she gestured with her hands back and forth between them.

"Look, he's sweet at first. Very kind and respectful. He asks one or two questions and finds ways to lead into more questions. The fact of the matter is that we don't know much about the family. We clean their house and they feed us and through them we live in a really nice apartment and can afford to do more things than we would without this job. But after a while, it turns into an interrogation. At one point, I told him I didn't know much about the family and didn't think it was appropriate to gossip about them to anyone. A week or so later, he asked me to lunch or dinner, I forget what it was, but by then, I didn't want to be treated like a spy, so I told him that it wasn't going to work out." Rachel had already started to notice the similarities between her experience and Jackie's.

"He has been curious but not to the extent that he was with you. I don't want to write him off just yet. If he starts to ask questions about the family on a regular basis, then I'll make a decision, but until then I think he's alright." She and Jackie finished up their lunch and changed the subject. As often as possible, they cooked within their apartment but on rare occasions, such as today, going to The Grill was a welcome change from routine. Getting up from the table the two of them began talking about the weekend. Both girls knew that their male peers within the complex would be sparse due to the gala this weekend. Neither of them had been given any drastic changes in their schedule. Rachel told her that on the day of the gala itself she was supposed to re-examine all the rooms for any hint of dust, dirt, or other flaw and to respond accordingly. Jackie would be leaving just before the gala began and would spend the majority of her shift assisting the staff with setting up the gala room and moving the more valuable paintings into that space as was usual for her.

Every year, the most valuable paintings that the family had accumulated over the centuries were put on display when the gala came around. It was known by the staff as well as the tour guides that during the first and second world wars the Smithsonian as well as other museums had contacted the family for storage purposes in order to keep the artwork safe from potential thievery. The government had dispatched a small security team of three men per conflict to stand guard in front of the room where the artwork would be stored. Based on the amazing food, recreational activities, and conversational treatment, the Skyler family had given the team during their stay, the men reported back that a piece of gratitude was due the family. As a token of appreciation following both wars, the family was permitted to keep about five pieces of their choosing per war. As a result, the family chose a work by DaVinci, two of Van Gogh and two from Botticelli each time they had the option. Among their repertoire of artwork, they had for an abbreviated period a statue of David. Apart from those that they were granted by the government, they already had a vast priceless collection of antique statuary and artwork dating back to the fifteenth century. Part of the reason for the security guard on the grounds of the estate was to keep the artwork safe. After each gala, the pieces were removed to an undisclosed private part of the house until the following year. The most important reason for the security team on the night of the gala was to protect the attendees against unwanted intruders. The event was always stage managed beautifully in the past but owing to it being a masquerade the need for security became obvious. Rachel and Jackie had just reached their cars when their respective phones went off. They turned to look at each other and answered. Words of affirmation followed by exchanges of puzzled glances prompted their re-entry to the bar for another round of conversation. Seated at the bar they groaned at the local comedian's antics on the stage. After waving off the bartender, the two women proceeded to compare phone calls.

"Mine was from Wendy," Jackie started.

"Mine too."

"The family decided to do a lottery this year and invite attendees to have a plus one," Jackie stated in monotone. Rachel stared at the bar in thought.

"Why are we invited to this thing?" Looking up to the comic on stage, Rachel grimaced as he began laughing at his own joke while some of the people yawned. She glanced at Jackie and asked again.

"Is it weird" – she shrugged – "that Wendy would have a pre-recorded message made up in advance to send?" Rachel wondered. Jackie stared at the poor guy on stage as people began to put money in the jukebox in order to drown him out.

"It doesn't surprise me, but it is unusual. Apart from never having gone to the gala before and hearing bits and pieces from those who have attended, what exactly are we supposed to do there?" Jackie asked aloud.

"Well, she said that the girls who were invited have dresses and masks that have been preapproved and should fit us, which again is weird and borderline creepy."

"Well, you can't ever say working there wasn't interesting." Jackie laughed. Getting there at nine that night wouldn't be difficult. It was the fact that the outfits in full were going to be delivered to their complex. They didn't need to go shopping for anything. That was a relief to Rachel especially.

"What exactly is the gala about?" Rachel asked. Jackie sighed.

"It's a silent fundraiser targeted at raising money for local causes that have nationwide significance." Rachel just stared at her.

"In layman's terms, that means what exactly?" she asked.

"Well, it means that the upper crust of society dresses up, hides their faces and at some point, in the evening anonymously donates some portion of money to a personally chosen charity that helps to fund the local school system, after school programs, the war vets. Anything having to do with the military is a huge concern to the family. Apparently, they have a long history of being involved in the nation's conflicts. The list goes on and on really. From homeless food shelters to endangered water mammals on the coast…it's a big deal," she finished.

"How can anyone donate to so many random charities in one night?"

"The people who attend have a vested interest in at least three of the charities being sponsored that night. This year, the family is placing emphasis on historical preservation along with a few other things."

"Historical preservation," Rachel stated. "What is there to preserve in Oregon?"

"I'm not sure but at least we get to dress up a little instead of wearing uniforms to work this time." Rachel nodded. Her phone lit up as Drew's name appeared on the screen. Jackie saw it and told Rachel she'd see her back at home.

"Hey, Drew," she said as she turned to see Jackie's car drive away.

"Hey, how are you?"

"Pretty good. Hey, I just found out I can take someone with me to this thing at work this weekend?"

"Oh yeah?"

"The dress code is pretty strict though and you have to wear a mask." Silence on the other end of the line was followed by laughter.

"What type of work are you doing over there?"

"It's a masquerade-themed fundraiser at the house. I have an outfit, but do you think you can find something by Saturday?"

She could hear the smile in his voice when he responded, "definitely." Talk turned to the day's activities with Rachel guiding the questions toward Drew.

She got in her car and told Drew she was driving back to the complex, but he suggested she meet him at the park.

Ten minutes later and a million thoughts ahead, Rachel arrived at the park. Joggers were making their rounds along with women and strollers. The usual Frisbee games, no-blood-no-foul basketball, and the broody readers lying beneath specifically chosen trees were a normal sight for Rachel. She walked over to a bench and sat down, not knowing when Drew would show up. As she sat and watched the families on their picnic blankets, she looked up to the sky. A beautiful blue sky with amazingly white clouds overhead mystified her. He followed her gaze to the sky above and watched her sit there and observe the parks attendants. She felt the hair on her neck stand up and looked across the park to see Drew standing beneath the shade of a tree, leaning against its center. She waved and he advanced across the open field. Walking in the middle of a few touch football games and dog Frisbee fetch he looked utterly focused on her. The sun shone against his olive skin. As he approached the bench and removed his sunglasses, the green eyes that continually took her breath away froze her in place. He sat down and for a few minutes, neither of them spoke. Just watching the people in the park seemed to be enough for them at the moment.

"A mask?" She nodded in response to him. Lost in thought, she kept thinking on the portrait above the fireplace on the residential floor. *The medallions*, she thought. That was it. The one thing all five had in common in the painting were the medallions they wore. She looked at him and asked if he could bring himself to go to a masquerade.

"I'm sure I can manage." He grinned. "When is it again?"

"Saturday. 9 PM. I don't really know what to expect. I was invited last minute."

"Hmm. You've never gone before?" She shook her head.

"Drew, where are you from?"

"I told you, I'm from a—"

"Little bit of everywhere," she finished. "But seriously where?" He looked away from her to the games and laughter in the park. He smiled and caught her eye.

"Why do you want to know?" he said with no emotion. She simply stared at him unable to move or to think. Her gaze shifted to the small metallic oval around his neck and back again to his eyes. He shifted his head to the side and asked again. Rachel began telling him about her discussion with Jackie that afternoon.

"Mhm" was his only response. Running his hand along the side of her face, he posed another question. "Who else is interested in me?"

"Richard." She stared blankly at him. He nodded.

"What does he know about me?" She proceeded to tell Drew about her conversation with Richie and stopped short at the intervention between her and Mrs. Skyler. Having been determined to get to know Drew she shook her head and blinked a few times. The look on Drew's face was stunned surprise.

"I think you owe me a few answers, Drew. If you don't start answering my questions and continue to poke and prod at the lives of the Skyler's through me, we won't have anything more to do with each other." She rose and walked to the jogging path. Being sure to stay in the walking lane. Drew sat in amazement on the bench and watched her walk away. He quickly joined her. She was clearly upset, and he would have to try a new tactic in order to get answers from her.

"Alright. Ask away."

"The medallion you have around your neck," she began without looking at him. Looking straight ahead, he realized she was refusing to make eye contact with him. *She's a smart one,* he thought.

"Yes?"

"Where is it from? I mean is it from a candy box, a friend, a family member?"

"A family member." He smiled. "I like this. What else?"

"You didn't answer my first question."

"Ah yes. Where am I from? Well that question could take some time to answer. But in simplest terms, I am from here." She stopped. For the first time, she looked at him and he smiled that mischievous grin that made her cave every time she saw it.

"Here? As in this little town? You don't sound like you're from here. The way you dress" – she gestured to his button-down shirt and jeans – "this is the first time I've seen you wear anything that resembles our age group. You almost always wearing black and you're lost in contemplation whenever I meet you for lunch or dinner. Considering this is the first time I—"

"Wow, wow, wow, wait a minute. You're analyzing my taste in clothes now. I wear black because I have a general dislike for doing laundry, so I went out and bought several shirts in the same color and wear them all the time because, guess what, their comfortable. As for being lost in thought, since when is thinking a crime." He spoke the last sentence in as much of a menacing whisper as he could without breaking into laughter. Rachel let out a frustrated sigh and continued moving along the trail. Meeting Drew and working for the family were the first signs of stability she'd had in her life. Not wanting to close the door on him completely she started in on a few harmless questions in the hopes that she could build up to more in-depth ones.

"Alright, you're from here," she began slowly. "But you haven't made this your permanent home. You're from other places so you like variety."

"I didn't hear a question." He stared at her as they walked. She kept her head down and her teeth had drawn in a corner of her mouth. "Chewing on your lips isn't healthy.

I noticed you chew on your cheeks at times as well, which also isn't healthy." She blinked and looked at him, still walking.

"Military?"

"No."

"Backpacker?" Drew laughed.

"Do I from time to time throw my belongings into a backpack and wander around foreign lands?" He raised his eyebrows. She looked at him and felt defeated. This conversation wasn't going to reveal anything new. "No, I'm not a backpacker."

"What can you tell me that's not vague about you?" she asked. They had reached another bench and he motioned for them to sit.

"I come from a close-knit family. They are from here. Unfortunately, I happened to be the one that didn't quite mesh with the family unit." Rachel narrowed her eyes.

"How is that not vague?"

"Vague by definition leaves things open to interpretation. I see no problem with having something be open to interpretation."

"How big is your family?"

"There are five of us initially."

"After this weekend, I think we should end our friendship. This isn't working." She started walking to her car. She felt a cold breeze brush past her and looked to see Drew leaning against her car. She stopped in her tracks and looked back along the path and then to her car again. She slowly approached him and whispered, "How did you do that?"

He dropped his sunglasses to the bridge of his nose and responded, "Do what?" He smiled and, in the time, it took her to blink he was gone.

Confused and aggravated by the lack of information he had given her, she arrived at Riverview to see most of the guys returning as well. She must have looked confused because she no sooner had shut her car door then Jordan approached her.

"You okay?"

"Yeah, I'm okay; I just have a lot on my mind."

"Okay because you were talking to yourself pretty adamantly and it looked a little." He made a circular motion next to his head with his finger.

"Ha-ha." She smiled. "You stink by the way." His shirt was soaked through with sweat and his face was sweltering. He grinned.

"Aww, you want a hug?" He attempted to wrap her into a sweat hug, but she weaseled her way away from him and up the stairs to her apartment laughing. Jackie was unzipping the dress bag and pointed to Rachel's without looking at her. She removed the light blue gown from its enclosed space and gasped. Hanging there on the wall, Jackie couldn't believe her eyes. The dress was cinched at the waist and cascaded to the floor looking like the opening of a flower. Rachel had just approached hers and turned at the sound of Jackie's reaction. Both stared on in admiration. The dress had an off-the-shoulder neckline and a skirt right out of Gone with the Wind. It was a sight to behold. The lace trimming along the neck gave the gown an added sense of prestige.

"Does the gala have a theme?" Rachel wondered. Jackie couldn't take her eyes off the dress. Finally, she looked up and responded.

"This year they chose to have civil war theme," she spoke with no emotion.

"Are you going to try it on?" Rachel asked. Both took deep breaths in.

"It's too beautiful to take off the hanger," she spoke still mesmerized. A little box sitting on the edge of the sofa caught Rachel's attention. Jackie followed her gaze and told her it was the mask for the gala. She opened the box to show Rachel and more 'wow's' and admiring glances were exchanged before laughter overtook them both. The mask would cover all but her mouth for that evening. It matched the gown perfectly and rather than lace had a black border. They had two days before the gala and they didn't want anything to happen to their gowns so they placed them in their respective closets. It was approaching three in the afternoon and the girls had wanted to run a few errands at the store before working out later. Leaving in Jackie's sedan, they took off for groceries.

Drew arrived back at his aged, brown, wood-paneled house overlooking a small pond. The trees and shrubbery overtook the property making the house look as though it were competing for its right to be there. He walked up the steps and through the front door absently shutting it as he went. After placing the keys in the metal container just inside the foyer, he advanced to the kitchen. The interior of his home was pitch black owing to the curtains being shut for the entirety of his stay. He preferred the dark and quiet feeling of his home. He passed through the kitchen noticing a coffee cup half filled with its contents and steam rising from it. Turning toward the hall, his shoes beat against the hard wood flooring and created an echo off the walls. His room was located furthest down the hall on the left. The door opened with a menacing creak. Approaching his closet, he found the suit and mask he was looking for. The tear in the right forearm of the suit made him grimace. He had waited for a long time to have an excuse to attend the gala.

"Sewing. At least, I learned something useful." He pieced together the old suit and put it back in the air locked space. He took his time moving through the house and found his way to the metal stairwell just outside the living room that wound down into the basement. The room was lit by over melted candles on long disused tables in the center of the room. The dust and dirt along the tables and on the stone floor was of no interest to him. The cobwebs flowing from the table and strung along the shelves were given brilliance by the light of the candles. He perused the walls of antique books lining the room. He approached The Art of War and pulled it toward him. The wall adjacent to him groaned and cracked open, unearthing dust and dirt from years of disuse. He pushed the wall inward and walked through. The wall swung shut after him and he reached for the iron torch on the wall. Pulling a lighter out of his pocket, he ignited the torch and walked down the arched stone hall. The floors, wall, and arched ceiling were all made up of the same hand dug stone. Moving further and further down the hall, he began to feel the cold air more intensely. Walking up the stairs before him, he arrived at a large oak door. Removing an age-old key from his pocket, he slipped it into the lock and turned it. The ironwork of the lock responded in kind and he pulled the door toward him. He placed the torch on the wall and walked through to the stone mantelpiece opposite the front door. The first floor remained untouched by time. The wooden floors, stonewalls, and long oak dinner table had remained unaffected in the fullness of time. The antique round top windows had the same silver hung drapes covering them. Over time, the drapes had become tattered and faded in sections. He climbed the wooden stairwell leading to the second floor. Of the four bedrooms, his had always been the first one on the right. The room had collected a fair share of webbing and dust in his absence, but he approached the window and pushed the drape aside. Through the thick trees, he could just make out the extended concrete balcony of the Skyler home. His mouth turned up in the corner.

"It's good to be home." He moved his hand and the room fell into blackness. Walking back downstairs, he approached the front door and stepped onto the thick wooden porch. He took a deep breath in and walked toward the lake, the underbrush moving away from him as he advanced. The lining of the lake was permanently covered in frost. He glanced around the circumference of the lake and placed one foot after the other in the water on the rim of the lake and disappeared from sight.

Chapter Four

Rick and Greg strolled through the airport with their leather luggage bags hanging from their shoulders. Both young men settled into the lounge of the terminal. Patty sat facing the window, looking over well-worn notebook pads. The notes within were legible and orderly; as she flipped the sheets over and over comparing them to each other she shook her head in frustration. The twins sat on either side of her. Sitting down the boys were about three inches taller than her. The height discrepancy was an old joke from years before, but to the twins it never got old. Rick twisted his wrist to check his watch and sighed staring out the window into the black of early morning. Greg adjusted the collar of his polo shirt and rested his head on his fist. All three were exhausted from traveling but going home produced just as much stress as it did relief. There were a few other passengers waiting in the lobby: notably two college co-eds ogling the twins. The women were on their way back to Oregon from New York. They sat in a row of seats in the lounge cattycorner to the Skyler's. *It was far enough away,* they thought, *to stare in wonder at the boys without being obvious.* Greg and Rick were gazing out the airport windows while Patty cross-referenced notepad after notepad. With her head still bowed, she glanced up from under her eyelashes toward the reflection in the window. The girls had been whispering incessantly and it had begun annoying her. The reflection in the windows showed that they were turning to each other and smiling and pointing ever so subtly at the twins.

Patty glanced back down at her notes and cleared her throat. The boys each had separate, but equally annoying habits of trying to entertain themselves in boring situations. For Rick, it was constantly checking his watch, cracking his knuckles, and popping his neck. Greg on the other hand would crack his back, his ankles even clear his throat a few times for good measure. Intermittently, they would glance around the airport to see if there was any decent entertainment to be had. Having listened to the cracking and popping for an agonizing ten minutes, she had had enough.

"Those girls look interested in you. Maybe you should go talk to them." The boys glanced over and back to each other. Patty resumed her studies. Without looking up again, she spoke.

"It was more of an urgent request than a polite suggestion." Rick and Greg stood up their full six foot four inches and set off toward the girls. Patty rolled her eyes as she heard the giggles of laughter produced by the twins' arrival. In about an hour or so, the plane would start boarding and, in that time, she would have to make sense of these journal entries. If there was one thing *he* had been meticulous about, it was recording his daily thoughts. Searching high and low all over the world, the three had only managed to locate five mangled journals that covered varying times. Piecing it all together was a momentous undertaking that she was more than willing to have assistance with.

She opened her laptop to check her e-mail and found a message in her inbox. It was dated a week ago and she didn't recognize the sender. She moved to delete it, but the title of the message got her attention. It read: Nice to see you. There was a link just beside the title indicating there was an attachment. She opened the email and the attachment began to download. The image was slowly becoming clearer on her screen and her eyes widened as it did so. It was a picture of her sitting in a café in New York drinking coffee perusing the journals. The picture was taken from a table just opposite her, close enough that she should have seen him but somehow didn't. The message below the image said: Don't stress yourself out. Mom could never read my writing either. See you soon. Andy.

Her heart began to race, and the twins looked across the lobby and saw her face in the windows. In an instant, they were at her side. Before they could ask a question, she pointed to the screen. Rick and Greg's faces became taught with ire. Greg's fists were clenched and shaking. Rick sat down for a second, just long enough to notice the steam coming from Greg's fists. Rick had been holding on to the chair edge tight enough to form a dent in the shape of his hand.

"Call Fred," Rick whispered to Patty. Patty blinked twice before shutting her computer to do as she had been told. She rose and walked down the terminal to make the call.

"You have to calm down, look," he said pointing to Greg's fists. Greg looked down and took a deep breath in.

"Patty's calling Fred which means the family will be told all about this in a matter of minutes."

"The counter," Greg replied in a low tone. Rick shook his head, confused.

"The counter. In the photo, you and I are standing at the counter ordering. He was right there. Looking at all three of us. How did we miss him?" Rick took a deep breath in and shook his head.

"We both need to relax; we can't get on the plane like this." Greg nodded. He looked over Rick's shoulder to the confused girls looking back and forth at each other.

"Right. Relax. Let's," he said walking back to the girls. Rick smiled and followed. Patty returned just as she saw the twins rejoining the girls. She shook her head and placed her laptop back in its bag. The journals were repacked, and Patty approached the boys. The co-eds were moments away from a make out session according to their thoughts. They seemed to share half a brain. As the twins closed the gap between each girl and themselves leaning in, Patty appeared at Rick's side. Rick kissed his co-ed and before kissing her, again made an inquiry.

"Yes?"

Patty sighed. "Fred wants updates while we're in the air. Emphasizing that we should have a guesstimate on his whereabouts and appearance by the time we touch down." The girls were increasingly annoyed at the interruption. Finally, Greg's co-ed untangled herself from him and spoke.

"Do you mind? They're a little preoccupied." She laughed and spoke with elongated annunciation. As she looked at Patty for the first time, she immediately began to feel her self-esteem dwindle into nothing. Patty was five foot eight with shockingly blonde hair and emerald green eyes. Her size two frame and pearly white teeth were a far leap from the girl's own appearance of bleached hair, blue-eyed contact lenses, and teeth that were beginning to show the early signs of smoking. Greg placed his hand around the girl's jaw line and drew it back to face him to continue. Rick and his choice were unaffected by the interruption.

"Is that all he said?" Greg asked as he resumed his leisure. Patty sat down in the row of chairs behind the foursome. Opening her bag, she began perusing the journals again.

No, she thought. "He also asked me to watch and make sure that the two of you don't cause trouble *in any way*," she emphasized. Both boys let out a light laugh. The girls looked confused but giggled in response. Greg's blonde was thinking about where they would go when things became more serious, assuming it would. Rick's blonde was designing her wedding gown and imagining the looks on the faces of her friends as she walked down the aisle to meet Rick. At this, Rick pulled away from her and gave a stern look over her shoulder to Patty. Patty smiled and looked up from her studies to see both boys glaring at her. She shrugged her shoulders and continued.

They can't help but think that way, she thought. "Besides I thought her dress was actually quite nice." The twins opened their eyes to look at Patty while maintaining contact with their entertainment.

You know, Patty, maybe you should give Reid another chance? Greg thought. Patty's thoughts turned to obscenities and Rick decided to settle the tension. He pulled away from his co-ed and asked if she wanted to walk a while through the terminal considering they'd be seated for a while. The girl's heart leapt in approval and all three Skylers groaned their thoughts in unison. Greg and his blonde took the same path down the terminal. Patty watched the four of them walk away.

Maybe I'll give you a play by play, Patty, Greg thought. Rick looked back at Greg and he responded with a look of innocence.

Trish said we couldn't do that anymore. It's rude, Rick thought. Patty's phone buzzed and she looked to see Reid's name on the screen. The twins were down the terminal walkway but it didn't stop Greg from responding.

"Oh come on, Patty, give him a chance." He laughed thoughtfully.

"Did you see the club they went to Greg? You may want to hold off any more serious contact with her. You never know where she's been," Patty responded.

"Even if she is sick, it wouldn't affect me. Maybe you should have Richie take a look at that hair of yours. I think the blonde is beginning to affect your—"

ENOUGH, Rick thought. "Can I please do this without the two of you bickering like always?"

"Sorry." They both glumly responded. The time passed in silence with the twins preoccupied and Patty sitting by the gate. She closed her eyes to think over all that had happened in New York. She pulled her camera out and began uploading photos of their visit. The announcement over the P.A. came for the plane to start boarding just as all the photos were done. Patty packed up her belongings and made her way to the stewardess checking the tickets. The twins returned and the girls looked exhausted. Greg's choice was awash with sweat from head to toe. She was flushed in her face and her eyes looked as though she were about to pass out. Greg gave her some water and Rick asked them where they were sitting. Luckily, Patty thought, they were sitting in a further section of the plane. The twins joined her at the gate, and they made their way down the walk to the plane. In silence, they found their seats with Rick giving up the window seat for Patty, Greg sitting in the aisle and Rick sitting between them. The girls sauntered by the trio and gave halfhearted smiles to the twins who smiled in return. The looks of sheer exhaustion on their faces almost made Patty feel sorry for them. With so few passengers, the plane was able to take off quicker than expected. Once they were in the air Patty opened her laptop to start looking through the photos. Greg caught the stewardess's attention and asked for water to be given to the girls that were sitting further back. Rick was looking over the photos with Patty when he sighed. Both Greg and Patty looked to him.

"Alright, ask," he said. Patty made no response. Greg looked to her and cleared his throat. She closed her eyes and sighed. Turning in her seat toward both boys, she responded.

"So how was your ride?" she asked in mocking derision. Rick started first. He clasped his hand over his face and groaned.

"She wouldn't stop planning her wedding. Then she started singing." He closed his eyes in exhaustion and Patty couldn't contain her laughter.

"Wait, mentally or out—" Greg asked.

"Out loud," Rick finished. Greg and Patty were doubling over in hysterics now.

"Wait a minute. What was her choice? No don't tell me. Britney? Christina? Oh I have it! Miley?" Patty's eyes were wide with amusement.

"Party in the U.S.A is not that great of a song and she only knew the chorus. She kept singing it over and over. It was unbearable." Patty had tears coming down her cheeks and Greg tried without success to muffle his laughter. Patty wiped the tears from her face and caught her breath. Rick took the laptop from Patty's tray and placed it on his own. While looking through them, Patty cleared her throat at Greg.

"What?" he asked. Both Rick and Patty looked at him and thought, *Come on, give it up*.

"Mine was actually okay. Not a whole lot going on upstairs. She, uh, hummed a lot. It was kind of cute." He shrugged. Rick and Patty simply stared at him.

"Okay! Fine! She kept thinking about a water slide park in Florida. The cool water was imprinted on her brain. Oh," he said glumly. "Never mind I get that," he said. He looked down at the floor and Rick and Patty were quick to cheer him up.

"One of these days, you'll find someone who can tolerate the heat, Greg. It'll happen," Rick assured him. Just as they were finished talking, they heard the girls start.

"I don't understand. It was overcast and crazy cold the whole time," Greg's choice said.

"Oh, sweetie, we'll get some aloe at the next airport. It doesn't look that bad." Rick's choice soothed her.

"Doesn't look that bad! I'm scorched from being in rainy New York. How is that not bad? It burns! I look like a tomato!" Greg's choice exclaimed. Both boys looked to Patty.

"No," she stated. Scrolling down the screen on her laptop looking at photos, the twins' thoughts were clear.

"Please?" Greg whispered. Rick nudged her with his elbow.

"This is the last time." She sighed. She stood up and inched past the two of them to the aisle. She walked down to the restroom past the girls. The burned girl had begun to whimper in pain. Patty passed the image to the twins. The girl had close to third degree burns on her body and if left unattended it could only get worse. She could feel the guilt coming from Greg as she moved to the restroom door out of sight of the girls. Patty closed her eyes and lifted her hand palm face down and angled toward the burned girl. The boys' eyes were fixed on the seats in front of them watching the process. No sooner had Patty exhaled than thick white ice came seamlessly from her hand enveloping the girl in its glacial embrace. Layer upon layer of unseen ice. To anyone watching it would look odd, but the Skylers could see the ice wrap itself around the girl and sooth the burns into nothing. Patty returned to her seat and Greg nodded. By the time the plane landed, the burns would be non-existent. Having looked over the photos for the duration of the flight and not finding a hint of anything they closed the laptop.

Patty had found repeated references to *his* mother in the journals. She pointed the fact out to the twins.

"Do you think *he* knows?" she asked them. The boys merely shrugged. "I mean we were all there. I know we all expected *him* to show, but *he* never did." Rick made a call to Fred just before they landed and informed him of the results of their search. Having found nothing in their photos or *his* journals that would lead to answers they were resolved to gather the family together and share information. Arriving sooner than expected worked in the Skyler's favor. Passing through the terminal, they saw Teddy leaning against the town car with a wide grin. After embracing each other and placing their bags in the trunk, they began the familiar drive back to the house. Teddy couldn't contain his excitement. Looking into the rearview mirror, he struck up conversation.

"It's great to have you guys back. We've been looking forward to it for some time now."

"How have you been, Teddy?" Greg asked. Patty yawned and Rick ran his fingers through his hair.

"I've been great! I tell you what, the family has been buzzing about your return since we heard yesterday morning." Patty's eyes met his and her jaw locked.

"She's back too? You've got to be kidding!" The boys had seen the image of the raven flash across Teddy's mind and were just as eager to be told the full story of Fred's ride to work that morning. Teddy hung his head and dropped his gaze from the mirror. Having told the trio all of what he saw and heard during the drive, the twins began to relax but the day was only just beginning. Turning onto the drive through the entrance gate the security guard shot a smile at the occupants and they responded in kind. Approaching the main gate, they saw Geoffrey speaking to the 'non-rez' security team at the foot of the stairs leading to the front door. Teddy opened the door for them, and the trio took their bags into the house. The security team watched the procession and when they were out of sight, Teddy appeared at the doorway to stare at them. Geoffrey sent the team onto their respective assignments and met Teddy as he touched the driver's door handle.

"How was their trip?"

"They seemed tired, but glad to be home. It's the first time I've seen them relax since Grace."

Inside, the trio gathered in the elevator climbing toward the residential floor. Fred and Trish were seated in front of the fireplace reading and sipping tea respectively. Once Patty, Rick, and Greg had disembarked the elevator, they were greeted with massive smiles and warm hugs. Following some talk about the flight, Fred told them about the meeting taking place that night. The trio placed their bags in their individual rooms and all five re-entered the elevator for the security floor. Geoff was waiting in the security room looking over the cameras one last time. With the sash in hand, he walked into the lobby and heard the door click shut behind him. The doors opened and the Skyler's emerged to see a grim-faced Geoffrey waiting for them. Down the hall, Richie and Wendy's footsteps could be heard echoing against the stonewalls. Joining the family in the lobby the last to arrive was Harrison. Patty and the twins couldn't contain their laughter. Harrison scowled in response.

"Richie? You bleached his hair?" Patty smiled inquisitively. Looking to Harrison, Richie shook his head in disapproval.

"He went against my advice I'm afraid and this is the result." He smiled at Patty and embraced her. Wendy embraced all three and inquired about their flight. Following the small talk, the group made their way to the couch and love seat. Geoff placed the sash on the table and the twins jumped up.

"At the risk of repeating a previous conversation, let's not jump to conclusions," Geoff spoke gruffly. Harrison stepped forward in alignment with Geoff and placed a purple rose on the table. The Skyler quintet regained their seats while Wendy, Richie, Harrison, and Geoff stood. While Patty and the twins remained fixated on the sash, the rest of the company were staring up at Geoff in response to the flower.

"I found it on her grave. No note. Just the flower." He sighed.

"When did the sash appear?" Patty asked.

"Yesterday morning. It was tied around the entrance gate." She simply nodded.

"The flower didn't show up on the cameras because it wasn't placed there until after two this afternoon." Fred had heard enough, as had the rest of the group.

"Obviously he's back. Now the question becomes what are we going to do about it?" Fred posed.

"I have a few ideas," Geoff responded, his temper clearly rising. Rick spoke for the first time.

"The gala is coming up this weekend. I trust the team is prepped for it. Do we think he'll try to get in?"

"I have doubled security. Just last year, we had two art thieves get in here before the team found them hovering around a few pieces. No mistakes this year. Invites were sent out specifically and will be checked thrice upon the arrival of the guests as will be the identification of the attendees," Geoff responded. Richie cleared his throat and Patty looked to him for the first time since sitting.

"Of course, you can do my hair and make-up. You've never done wrong by me especially when it comes to public appearances." Richie simply smiled in response.

"I'm glad you have such a fervent trust in my unparalleled skills. However, I have something else to share. I think that he has been attempting to get in by using a female employee or two." Trish recalled the conversation she had with him earlier in the day. He had regaled her with the discussion he had with Rachel. In turn, he now regaled the group with the same tale. Greg was being swathed with ice from Patty. Rick and Fred remained calm.

"I understand that she and Jackie have been invited to the gala." Geoff turned to Wendy. She nodded.

"I wanted to draw him out, and by inviting Rachel and giving her the option of inviting a plus one, I can only assume she would ask him to attend with her."

"Okay so let me get this straight. We are using this girl as bait so that he can get into the house and then what? We have become stronger over the years and it wouldn't be that much of a stretch to believe he has as well. Perhaps he has new abilities than when we saw him last. What then?" Rick was postulating every theory that popped into his head.

"I'm not okay with Jackie being invited. The girl has problems," Greg said. "Last time I saw her, she was staring at that photo of us hunting the deer. She was just staring at it. It was creepy. Then when she saw me, it was like Christmas day in her brain. The word salivating came to mind when she looked at me, it was gross."

"If I didn't invite both her and Jackie, it would have created a rift between the girls. No one will be paying attention to Jackie anyway," Wendy explained.

"What's the theme this year anyway?" Geoff asked.

"Civil war," Wendy stated. The Skyler trio grimaced at the collected company.

"You can't be serious," came the reply from Patty. "You may as well tell him to come in his old suit and that ridiculous cape. He's a hoarder through and through. Never throws anything out. His journals make repeated references to his possessions and I think his clothes from that night are, in all likelihood, still in mint condition. Who's this Rachel and why are you so fascinated by her, Richie?"

"If you must know, I think she'd make a good match with either of you boys." The twins sighed in unison and changed the subject. Richie saw the airport entertainment flash through the heads. He started laughing uncontrollably. Mr. and Mrs. Skyler looked at the twins in stern disapproval. Fred spoke for the first time.

"We have more important matters to discuss and think about than your unorthodox approach to dating." He looked at the twins. The boys smiled at Fred and he grinned in response. "Really, Greg, don't beat yourself up; years ago you would have set her completely on fire. Look how far you've come." Greg's face brightened at Fred's words.

"Honestly, the three of you. This 'boys will be boys' approach to life is becoming ridiculous. The two of you will not behave that way again. I have told you repeatedly that treating all women, not just the ones that are from this family, with respect is a must, not a recommendation!" Trish had raised her voice for the first time in years. The boys were staring at her in shock. The walls around the group began to shake and the weather outside turned into a full-fledged hurricane. Geoff raised his arms and let them fall to his sides in exasperation. He and Harrison shook their heads, but Geoff had heard enough.

"That's it!" he raised his voice above the calamity. With his words, Trish calmed herself and the house as well. The weather outside returned to its normal state and the security team on the grounds looked to each other in confusion. The group remained quiet for several moments. The security door clicked open. Several of the men within popped their heads around the corner to see if all was really calm or if they should take cover somewhere in case that was just a warmup. Geoff cleared his throat and the men looked to him and disappeared back into the office.

"How do we know when the rose was left?" Wendy asked.

"The cemetery is the only piece of land on the estate without video recording. The last time someone was there, it was two in the afternoon," Geoff responded. "The bottom line is, we are prepared for him and any of his potential friends that may stop by for the gala."

"The journals are full of references to his mom. We only found five journals, so there's no telling how much information we're missing. I do know that the information we have is choppy. One of them starts from the beginning; the next from two years ago; and the rest are fairly vague when it comes to the time period," Patty chimed in.

"So we don't know what he looks like, where he is, what his plans are and we've invited him to the gala. Did I leave anything out?" Fred asked. The group shook their heads.

"The next time you schedule a meeting with us come with facts that are pertinent, not scattered, and incoherent."

"Yes, sir," Geoff said. The five departed for the elevator while the rest of the group made their way to their respective exit through the original family portrait.

Upstairs Reid was standing in front of the fireplace on the residential floor. Staring into the flames, he thought back on Grace's will to him. He hadn't been to the bank yet to retrieve whatever was in the safety deposit box, but he couldn't bring himself to visit her grave yet either. He picked up a frame on the coffee table containing candid shots of Grace with the family before it all went wrong. The elevator doors opened, and he placed the frame back in its place turning just in time to see the Skyler's walking down the hall to their rooms.

"Welcome back," he whispered. The boys turned and acknowledged him with a nod of their heads. He would see them all tomorrow and he knew they were in need of rest, so he walked down to the security floor where his room was waiting and collapsed onto his bed.

Patty pushed the curtains aside and looked up to the sky. She hadn't been home since Grace's funeral. Even then, the anger and tension that permeated the house made sleep a rare commodity. Greg settled into his room and breathed out a sigh of relief. He sat down at his table and looked through the family album lying there. Grace had left it to him. Covered in dust, tattered, and falling apart, the album was held together with drawstring tied together by Grace herself. He flipped the cover over and would have cried if he were capable. The pain in his eyes radiated through the rest of his body. He flipped the cover shut and retied the album. He lay down on the bed and closed his eyes. Rick was up for another hour looking out the window at the sky and the tree line just as Patty had done. Sadness was something he had become accustomed to. The life the family lead was not one for the faint of heart and having the family together even under hostile circumstances was better than not having them at all.

Rick rubbed his hands over his face and lay down to sleep for the night. The trio fell asleep just as Fred and Trish did. The house was going to be under lock and key for the next seventy-two hours and the residents therein felt safer than they had in a while. The security patrol along the gates and grounds as well as the interior patrols were on alert. Geoff had made it clear that this weekend there were not to be any screw ups.

Heads would roll, Jordan thought. That's what Geoff had told them. *Any mistakes and heads would roll.* The night had become bitter with cold. He walked back along the tree line making up the rear border of the house. Walking parallel with the house now, he could see a security member through the window. Reaching the other side of the house, he heard a noise coming from the woods. He could just make out the trail leading to the cemetery. Scanning the tree line, he didn't see anyone, but he could tell that something was definitely there. The voice in his earpiece cleared its throat. He turned to see Cam at the further end of the front of the house.

"Watcha doin'?" he asked. Jordan turned his gaze back to the trees for one last look. He turned finally and walked up to the front yard where Cam had reached around the corner to see him.

"Thought I saw something."

"Yeah, we call that wildlife." Cam smiled.

"Can never be too careful."

"In other words, Geoff scared you to death." Jordan looked him in the eye with genuine fear.

"He said heads would roll." Cam laughed.

"You think he's gonna come after you with a machete." Jordan started to walk away.

"I know for a fact he has a saber," he whispered over his shoulder.

"Ladies, would you like some hot cocoa to go along with your social hour," came Geoff's gruff voice over their earbuds. Both men turned to stare up at the camera. They shook their heads in unison.

"No, sir." They turned from each other and went along their routes.

"A saber," Cam whispered. "It's probably a useless piece a crap from the great war or somethin'." As he walked along the perimeter of the house, he heard a muffled noise along the trees. He approached the tree line and turned his flashlight on. Moving the light left to right, he scanned the trees but didn't see anything. He shrugged. He turned to resume his route and froze in place, wide-eyed, the tip of the saber touching his throat. Geoffrey leaned in close enough for Cam to see the whites of his eyes.

"Does it feel like a piece of crap, Son?"

Cam opened his mouth to respond but failed to form any words.

"Great war? Do me a favor and don't speak unless you have a job-related reason to do so. Ya got me!" Cam nodded slowly. He blinked and Geoffrey was gone. He breathed out for the first time in minutes and placed his hand over his chest.

Geoff reappeared in the security office. The screens on the walls all showed the same images of blank property. Geoff looked across the room at the computer screens. The guys were still beating themselves up over the bow and the rose. Having missed both items on camera, they focused on the monitors like hawks surveying land for signs of movement.

Chapter Five

The next morning, Trish skipped breakfast with Fred and descended the stairs for her office. The twins and Patty had woken earlier and were sitting in the drawing room just beside the balcony while Fred sat alone outside reading the paper with Reid. Patty stared up at the painting above the fireplace. Greg watched Trish descend the stairs and turned to follow. While Patty absorbed herself in journals, Rick decided to take a stroll downstairs as well. As soon as they reached the first floor, they saw Jackie absently dusting a table while staring at an old photo of them. Greg rolled his eyes and casually walked by her toward the kitchen. Rick made his way to the planning room. Jackie jumped in shock as the boys passed her by. She watched them as they walked and opened her mouth but only a tiny incoherent babble emerged, and Greg stopped to look at her while Rick continued on. Jackie closed her mouth and stared wide-eyed at Greg. He approached her slowly and her heart raced with each step he took.

"Good morning." Jackie just stared back at him.

"Uhuh" was her high-pitched response. Greg shook his head. He decided to try again.

"I understand you're going to the gala." Jackie summoned her courage and tried to say something back.

"Yes. Are you?" Instantly, she regretted it. *He lives here you twit*, she thought to herself. Greg felt something close to pity for her. But only momentarily. He hated it when women started planning their wedding to him. *This is exactly why I avoid talking to her*, he thought.

Then end the conversation, came Rick's response.

"Yeah, I'm going," Greg responded.

"Cool," she replied. Greg walked away and made a beeline for the kitchen. He could smell the cinnamon rolls from upstairs. Jackie breathed out all the air in her and felt her knees regain some of their strength. She had a huge grin on her face by the time she saw Rachel descending the stairs. She ran up to her and nearly knocked her down. Rachel stared wide-eyed at her.

"What is it? What?" She laughed. Jackie could hardly contain herself. She pointed toward the hall leading to the kitchen. Rachel's eyes followed the direction and returned to Jackie's face.

"The twins," she whispered, "they're back!" Rachel blinked.

"Okay?" she responded. Jackie's eyes became wide.

"One of them spoke to me. On purpose." Rachel laughed.

"Not uh! What'd he say?" She moved to go down the hall for breakfast in the kitchen. Jackie followed. She regaled her with the conversation as if the FBI recorded it. Not one blink, grin, or tilt of his hair was left out as they made their way to Maggie's breakfast. Wendy watched his face change to an expression of curiosity. Listening to

Jackie's story as they approached the kitchen door, Rachel felt compelled to see Wendy. She had stopped listening to Jackie and had begun walking toward the planning room. Jackie stopped talking and watched Rachel walk away. Rachel only heard the faint echoes of Jackie's voice calling her name. Jackie shrugged and went into the kitchen where a few seats were still open at the table. Having at last approached the doorway of the planning room Rachel peeked inside to see one of the twins and Wendy staring back at her. After a moment of awkward silence, Wendy cleared her throat and raised a question.

"Yes, dear?" Rachel simply stared at Rick without responding. Greg looked to the kitchen door having seen Rick's situation in the planning room. Rick looked absently back at her before passing her on his way to the security offices below. She made an attempt to say something but stopped short having thought better than to make a fool of herself. She turned slightly to watch him walk down the hall.

"Hello? Rachel!" Wendy was still wondering what she was doing in the doorway instead of eating. Rachel jumped at Wendy's voice. In a daze, she looked back to Wendy then glanced to the floor. She turned slowly to go to the kitchen. Wendy followed her as far as the doorway to make sure she was all right. Rachel pushed the door open and was saturated in the smell of sweet cinnamon as the pile of cinnamon rolls on the table greeted her. Wendy glanced down the hall in the direction Rick had traveled and saw him leaning against the wall. He looked over to Wendy and turned the corner. Venturing toward the portrait of a wide oak tree with the sun glinting off a lake in the background he glanced back once more and saw Wendy standing at the corner as he had. Having pushed the portrait in, he stopped short of going through and simply stood in the frame.

"Yes?" he asked. Wendy face remained unchanged.

"I saw that." Rick continued through the passage and walked down the stone steps to Geoff's office.

In the kitchen, the morning group had officially assembled around the table, but due to their unannounced visitor they all stared and ate instead of conversing. Greg simply stared back at them as they ate. Every so often, he would talk to Steve or Maggie and look toward the painting of the man and the lake on the wall. He was leaning against the stove turning an apple over in his hands. Rachel stepped through the door and took her seat at the table. Seeing the room so quiet was unsettling to her. She looked around the table at her peers noting the clearing of throats, staring at plates and the sideways glances to one another. Jackie sat beside her looking intently every so often to the right. Rachel took a roll off the center plate and followed Jackie's gaze. Greg was used to being stared at to the point that he had become somewhat vain. Having seen Rachel take her place at the table he watched her eat. She began to look warily at her peers. Looking at Rachel, he became more and more frustrated.

"So how has everyone's day been?" she asked. Apart from the switching of pans from one burner to another and the stream of conversation among the kitchen staff, the room had been oddly silent. Jackie turned to Rachel and attempted to make a reply but was stopped short.

"Are you Rachel?" Greg asked. His voice lacked any intonation. All eyes on Rachel she simply nodded. Greg continued to stare at her.

"I don't mean to be rude, but I don't know the difference between you and your brother. What's your name?" she spoke slowly. The eyes of the room went from one to the other as they spoke as if following a tennis match. Greg's face remained set as if made of stone.

"Greg," he responded.

"Nice to meet you." She glanced down at her breakfast and Jackie saw an opportunity.

"I'm Jackie. We met in the hall a little while ago." Greg looked blankly at Jackie inclining his head slightly. He put the apple on the table and left the room making his way to the security offices. Walking out the door, he was greeted by Wendy. She stood in the hallway with a knowing stare fixed on him. Greg looked back at her with confusion.

"Why so intrigued?" she asked.

"Intrigue implies interest. She's plain, lacks any kind of thought."

"Ah so staring at her and speaking to her before anyone else in that kitchen apart from Steve and Maggie means you're completely uninterested in plain-Jane, thoughtless Rachel."

"Exactly. You should try the rolls. Everyone in there loves them." He proceeded around the corner to the security offices below but changed his mind as he approached the painting and walked back down the hall to the stairwell in the foyer. In the kitchen, the table was awash with excitement and speculation. The girls were all buzzing about Greg especially Jackie. The boys wondered if Patty was back as well. No one had seen her yet. Reid emerged from the painting on the wall carrying a food tray from Mr. Skyler's breakfast. Hearing the commotion, he gathered that Greg had been in the kitchen. The moment he sat down, the boys began their interrogation.

"Have you seen her? Is she back? Is she still hot?" The questions went on and on before Maggie had heard enough. Between the fixation on Rachel and now Reid's interrogation, she slammed the oven shut and the room went silent.

"If you all have nothing better to do than gossip about the members of this family, then you can leave. Do you have other things to do? Well?" The room made muffled apologies. Maggie collected herself and resumed her work. The employees slowly resumed their talks about the weather, movies, the gala the next day, and so on. Rachel's question had been answered by some of the staff. After breakfast, the buses started pulling up to the front entrance of the house. As they filed toward the foyer, Jackie and Rachel parted ways as Rachel made her way back up the stairwell. Her thoughts had been on Rick since she saw him before breakfast. Now Greg caught her interest as well. *The two of them look exactly identical*, she thought. *I've seen twins before, but they always had some kind of idiosyncrasy to distinguish themselves from one another.* Still thinking about the boys, she walked into Richie at the head of the stairs without seeing him. Richie caught her as she began to fall back toward the stairwell. Her eyes wide with fear he caught her by her arms and pulled her upright. She breathed a sigh of relief.

"Thank you." Her heart began to calm down as Richie nodded and resumed his walk down the stairs. She pulled the vacuum from the closet door and emerged to find one of the twins sitting in a chair in the drawing room. He sat there reading a book. His back was to her as she entered the room. She looked at the painting and then back at him. It was an exact replica. Paintings from the civil war era were seldom accurate about their subjects. Having gone to college as an art history major, she knew that each subject's best feature or worst flaw was ironed out or exaggerated as the artist saw fit. To see him sitting there was as if he was sitting in front of a mirror.

"Excuse me?" He made no sign of having heard her. Rachel subtly cleared her throat. Still nothing. Richie had retraced his steps up the stairwell and saw what Greg was doing. Not wanting to intervene too early, he decided to watch it play out. Rachel didn't know what else to do. She didn't want to make a commotion and upset him but on the other hand she didn't want to leave without finishing her work for the day. She left the vacuum in the hall and returned with a duster in hand. Quietly going about her job, she began with the mantelpiece then to the tables. Retrieving her mini vacuum, she tended to a few spots on the curtains over the windows. He had glanced up once or twice as she went around the room.

"How long have you worked here?" He hadn't looked at her for the question and he wouldn't look up for the response. She had stopped working on the curtains to answer his question.

"About a month. When did you arrive?" He kept reading and without looking up made his reply.

"Early this morning." She turned to finish the curtain and then left the room for the vacuum. She came back into the room with it this time and plugged it in.

"I have to vacuum so it may get a little noisy." He closed the book and stood to leave the room. As he did so, she saw his cufflink. With the fire going and the room being so dark due to the poor weather outside, his cufflink had been made brilliant by the flames. He noticed her stare.

"Was there something else?" She glanced from his wrist to the painting briefly. He followed her gaze. Richie decided it was time to intervene. Just as he entered, she made her response.

"Are those common? A guy I know has one, but he wears it around his neck." Greg's face became taught as he flipped his wrist palm face up to glance at the medallion he had sewn there. He looked up to see her face turn to one of worry. Richie caught his eye.

"Rachel, have you finished this room yet? The tour groups are coming in about ten minutes." He looked from Rachel to Greg and back to Rachel. The two of them stared at each other without a word.

"Her boyfriend has something that looks like my cufflink apparently."

"Here's a question," Richie started "Why are you wearing cufflinks at 8:30 in the morning?" Greg looked to Richie as if he had been slapped upside the head. Rachel could feel the tension between Richie and Greg building.

"He's not my boyfriend."

"It's not really a cufflink. It's supposed to look like a button on my sleeve."

"Then maybe you shouldn't call it a cufflink." Rachel began to feel herself turn invisible. The two men talked as if she weren't there.

"Umm. Excuse me. He's not my boyfriend."

"Does it look like a cufflink?"

"A little. But on the whole, it's a button."

"HEY!" Both men stopped and looked at Rachel. She felt the heat rise in her face and immediately regretted yelling. Richie looked at Rachel and she felt her heart race faster than ever.

"I'm sorry. That was out of line. I do need to finish this room but I was waiting for" – she looked to Greg and then back to Richie – "the room to be unoccupied so that I wouldn't bother anyone." The two of them continued to simply stare at her. Both looked as though they were getting more and more frustrated as they stared at her.

"Also—"

"He's not your boyfriend," they finished. Richie took a step toward her. Rachel felt unable to move.

"What does your friend's necklace look like?" She glanced up at the portrait on the wall, then to Greg's wrist and back to Richard. The two men exchanged glances and looked to Rachel.

"I see," was Richard's only response. "Well, we'll leave you to finish the room." With that, the two of them left and walked up the stairwell. Greg gave one last look at Rachel and disappeared up to the third floor. She breathed out a sigh and shook her head.

Upstairs, Greg and Richie were in deep conversation with Rick. "I can't hear her," Greg commented.

"Maybe that's a good thing," Rick replied. He lacked any emotion in his face or voice.

"There's something about her," Richie added. The three of them couldn't put their fingers on it but there was something there.

"Don't mind me," came a voice from the balcony. "Just trying to put pieces together from a few journals spanning an amazing amount of time with no connection to each other whatsoever apart from the author. By myself." The boys looked toward the double doors and resumed their conversation. No sooner had they started talking than the raven flew by the windows and landed on the balcony wall.

"Why can't we hear her?" Greg asked. "I mean we've been around awhile and everyone's been an open book."

"I agree. It is strange. She is easily persuaded though. She told me all about him yesterday. Today, however, she seems stronger. Maybe she's started to figure it out," Richie said.

"What makes you say that, Richie?" Greg asked. Rick and Greg were equally curious.

"Because he tried to use Jackie to get re-acclimated with the family and everything about the workings of the house. Now he's honed in on Rachel. He told Rachel that Jackie was boring and that the house was a hive. I think he's overwhelmed which could mean that he's alone."

"Don't be ridiculous. She's worked here a month. The odds of her understanding all of this" – he waved his hand around the room – "is minimal to none," Rick responded.

"Don't underestimate her. I don't think he does," came Greg's response.

"Boo-hoo, I feel so sad for him. Maybe we should invite him over for coffee to make friends and then accidentally kill him," Rick replied. Greg laughed. The vacuum turned off downstairs and they heard Rachel descending the stairs for the first floor. The buses had pulled up and were taking the next shift back to their apartments. Richie approached the line of windows overlooking the front of the property.

"He makes friends like bees flock to honey. If he finds her to be a challenge and furthermore finds someone else in this house or more than one someone that could be to his advantage" – he looked back to the twins – "then we could be in real trouble here. So could Rachel for that matter." He watched her board the bus and turned away from the window.

"Look, I already spoke to Geoff and there is no way he could get on the property without us knowing. Don't worry. I'm not," Rick spoke as calmly as he could, but it didn't dissuade Richie from being concerned. Greg walked out to the balcony to join the girls in their journal work. Rick moved to glance out the window. Richie saw the look on his face.

"So that's what Wendy was talking about."

"What?" Rick sounded bored.

"You and Rachel?" Rick looked toward Richie.

"She smells like violets," he said. "And there is no 'and'." Rick spoke with a hint of frustration. Richie left him standing there and descended the stairs. The buses drove away, and Rick walked out to the balcony. Leaning against the wall, Greg poured over a journal while Patty sat at the table doing likewise.

"So, you are back," Rick spoke with indifference. She looked up from her journal and nodded. All three had delved into their respective journals. She straddled the wall but made no attempt at conversation. Patty was glad for the help but nervous at her arrival. The chair opposite Patty remained empty. Rick took the opportunity to sit and pulled a journal toward him.

"He's closer than you all think," she said without looking up from her journal. "This one's" – she nodded to the book in her hands – "from right after it happened. Grace is prevalent in almost every thought."

"How close is he?" Rick responded. She glanced up and out toward the tree line where the cabin stood.

"Not sure but he's definitely close." Greg turned the pages over and over in quick succession.

"Speed reading is obnoxious," Rick commented.

"So's your face."

"If the two of you can't sit here and help me figure this out, then maybe you should go look around the house. Amuse yourselves in some way." Putting their heads down they resolved to read through the journals and determine what they could from them. She kept looking toward the cabin in thought. Eventually, she decided to have a closer look. She tossed the journal to the table. Throwing her legs off the wall, she let herself fall into the air and just as she approached, the ground changed to a raven. The trio watched her fly out over the trees. The weather was especially bad. No sun, just rain and more rain. The cold air was beginning to permeate the house. More and more fireplaces were being lit and the staff would hover around them.

Trish sat in her office going over the final plans for the party tomorrow night. She looked up to the window to see the raven flying toward the lake. Turning from the window, she found Reid standing in her doorway.

"I've decided to go to the bank today. I have someone covering my shift. I told Wendy but I thought I'd tell you as well." Trish nodded and resumed her work. Wendy walked in as Reid departed. She brought the menus for the dinner after the gala. Reid walked out the front door just as the last bus was about to depart.

Jackie and Rachel arrived at their complex having not said a word to each other throughout the drive home. Well, Rachel hadn't said more than a few affirmative responses to Jackie's incessant chatter about the twins. Having spoken to Greg twice in one day and seen Rick up close, Rachel was beginning to see the fascination Jackie held for them. Slightly dazed they entered their apartment.

While Reid rode back with the nons, he managed to find a seat up by the driver. He had asked him to stop at the bank after he dropped off the last person. The chatter in the bus was at an all-time high. The Skyler's arrival at the house had caused so much excitement that most had forgotten about the gala the next day. While few apart from the security staff and a few non-resident women had been invited, all the employees enjoyed hearing tidbits about the preparations for the event. The last drop off was followed by a quick stop at the bank. He thanked the driver and the customers as well as some of the employees stopped and stared at the man departing the Skyler bus system. Reid approached the counter and asked to be given his safety deposit box. After exchanging papers with the manager, he was shone through a double door entryway into a private room. Left alone with the last thing left to him by Grace, he simply stared at the long grey metal box.

The waters on the lake began to ripple violently and, on the edge, Drew re-appeared with a look of resolute anger in his eyes. Passing through the overgrown grass, vines, and shrubbery leading to the cabin his mind was racing. The undergrowth arched away from him as he made his way into the house just as she landed on the roof of the cabin. The gala was tomorrow and that would be his prime opportunity. *If it's there, I'll find it*, he thought. He retraced his steps down the stone hall, torch in hand, and found his way back to the house. Having seen him come up from the water, she wanted further proof and had materialized on the porch just as he departed down the stone walkway. Once in the basement, the door shut behind him. Alone in the web-ridden, dust covered room he looked over the bookshelves. He approached the north wall and pulled a journal toward him. He perused it and placed it back on the shelf. He pulled another and another until the table was filled with them. He had looked through them all and still had no idea where to find it. He went back upstairs. She had kept quiet as she heard him tearing through the books on the shelves, listening from behind the passage door. After he left the room, she entered and saw the piles of journals lying on the table. Her eyes became wide with anticipation. Not knowing where she actually was, she took as many as she could carry and escaped down the passage once more to the hard wood door at the cabin. She made repeated trips from the basement to the cabin's kitchen table. Over and over, she swept down the passage until all the journals she had seen were there before her. She had no idea what information lay there so she walked out onto the porch and transformed in the blink of an eye. She made a beeline for the balcony and saw Patty sitting there as if made of stone. The boys had gone, but she knew she had to tell someone. Patty looked up as the raven showed no sign of slowing. As she landed on the balcony wall, she glided to the tabletop and started telling Patty about what she saw. Patty placed the journal on the table.

"You know you're still a bird, right?" Reid appeared in the doorway. He carried an antique wood box in his hand. She had ignored Patty and continued telling her what she'd seen at the cabin. Reid put the box on the chair and chuckled.

"Quote the Rav—" She transformed before he had the opportunity to finish and had pinned him to the wall. Her hand held a vice grip at his throat.

"Don't finish that sentence," she spoke softly, slowly but with such an eye-piercing glare as to make Reid definitively scared for his life. Patty took the journal from the table and began looking through it again. Patty cleared her throat.

"You know when you get angry or excited, you talk faster than anyone can comprehend. Can you start over?" She released her grip from Reid's throat and he let out a few coughs and rubbed his neck feeling his pulse return to normal. He took the box in hand and sat down at the table as she leaned against the balcony wall.

"After I left you, I peeked around the old cabin. I circled it a couple times and landed on a tree branch where these two cute little squirrels were having a pretty tense argument." Reid and Patty exchanged glances. She sighed.

"I digress. Anyway, while I was perched there, he appeared from the lake and looked fairly nonplussed if you ask me. After he went in, I moved to a windowsill on the porch. He disappeared behind an old oak door. After he didn't come back, I ventured inside myself." Patty grew tenser with each word she spoke. The twins returned to the balcony and greeted Reid. Patty caught them up on the story. She continued. The twins leaned against the wall opposite her.

"I opened the door and there was this long stone tunnel. I don't know where it led to, but it was very cold and very dark. It went on for quite a while before I came upon a firm wood surface. It was flat and cold like the tunnel. I could hear him on the other side. He was rummaging through what sounded like books, but he kept throwing them somewhere and I could hear them land with a thud here and there. At points, he threw them with such emotion that I heard the pages rippling through the air as the book would land with a meshing sound." The twins had heard enough and moved to leave and see for themselves what she had. She sped ahead of them and blocked their path.

"I wasn't finished. I heard him leave and pushed the wall. I found myself in a really very unkempt room. There were cobwebs, dirt, and dust everywhere. Not a light to be had either. Definitely a basement somewhere. All over a table and strewn on the floor were these thin books. Some looked quite aged while others could have been purchased last week. At any rate that I could summon, I picked up a pile and hauled them back to the cabin." The Skyler's eyes grew wide and Reid sat to attention. Patty opened her mouth to speak but she held her hand up.

"There all in the cabin sitting on the dining table—" The twins had bolted before she could finish. Patty sped after them. Whirling down the stairwell to the hall, they ran into Richie. Without explanation, they continued on their path. They made a beeline for the garage adjacent to the house. Tree cover, vines, and overgrowth of bushes and grass shrouded it. First out was Patty on her blood red and muddied dirt bike. She whipped around the corner of the house spraying mud at the security patrols while her hair lashed out behind her. The rain had begun to beat down harder on the ground as she made her way to the tree line behind the house. From the balcony, she and Reid watched as the trio tore into the forest with three handcrafted dirt bikes. They found the path leading toward the cabin and sped through the woods as fast as they could push their bikes. Kicking up mud behind them, the security team was baffled and mud covered looking into the trees. Wiping the grime from their faces, some of the team scowled.

"Damn trust fund, kids," growled one.

"Must be nice," said another.

As they approached the porch, they looked around for any signs of him. She appeared perched on the porch railing. The three were soaked through their clothes and cautiously crept up to the cabin door. Each peeked through a window. She transformed and led the way inside. Patty and the twins looked around the room as she moved toward the imposing door on the wall. The three stopped at the dining table and looked in surprise at the pile of journals lying there. They each carried a backpack and shoved as many as they could into them. Rick stopped and looked toward the door. He slowly placed the bag on the floor and walked toward the entrance to the tunnel. She was waiting by the door and opened it. All four froze. With a deep breath in, he stepped into the tunnel and found the torch on the wall. He gestured for a lighter and Greg handed him one. They proceeded slowly down the hall noting the temperature drop with each step they took. After a length, they reached the wall she had told them about. He leaned toward the wall listening for any hint of a sound. Having heard nothing, he pushed the door open and found the basement. All four of them stood in the tunnel hall. She pushed through them and walked in. She ran her finger across the table and made a look of disgust at the result. Rick placed the torch on the wall and the three stepped inside. They looked around at the nearly empty bookshelves. Greg inclined his head toward the winding metal stairwell in the corner. They walked toward it and looked up. Patty moved to step onto it, but Rick grabbed her arm and shook his head. Instead, Rick went up the stairs and arrived in the living room. He moved into the kitchen and heard rustling in a back room. Carefully, he crept down the hall but was quickly joined by the other three. The sound abated and he opened the door revealing a bedroom. They ventured in and found the room to be harmless. One of the windows had been left open and the wind had kicked up the pages of a book lying on the bed. They closed the door and quietly inspected the rest of the house. Pitch black throughout and the only sign of life was a coffee cup placed next to the kitchen sink. Wanting to know where they were, Rick led the group toward the front door and opened it. Stepping onto the front porch the first sight was trees and more trees. No sound of highway or traffic. They stepped onto the gravel drive and looked at the house for the first time. It looked as though it belonged more to the trees surrounding it than to any one person unfortunate enough to live in it. She changed without hesitation and flew up to the treetops. She could see the ocean and a few miles away, she could make out the town. She rejoined the group almost as soon as she had left them.

"The ocean's just through those trees." She pointed.

"Well, these tire tracks lead in the opposite direction." Greg noted.

"If he is living here, I don't want him to know anyone's been visiting," Rick said. Patty started following the tire tracks. The gravel wound its way through the woods and finally met an old highway. Patty found her bearings.

"I know where we are," she whispered.

"And," the rest prompted.

"The campgrounds are just through those trees about a mile or so. Well, the original ones anyway. Before the town was populated, we lived just through there. Don't the two of you remember?" The twins showed signs of only slight recognition. Patty crossed the old highway and entered the woods. Followed by the other three, she made her way to an old clearing. Here and there, wildflowers had sprouted up, but it was definitely the place she remembered. They could hear the water from the ocean and the birds in the trees talking to each other. It was their first permanent home. The boys approached an over gown hill of brush and thick tangled vines. Pushing through the mass of overgrowth, the boys discerned a house frame. The rot to the foundation had destroyed the house and over time, it had become almost unrecognizable as a former home. Patty watched the boys disentangle the roots and earth that had overtaken the house. It wasn't much to look at, but the remnants of the house brought back memories of happier times. The boys were unearthing the stone foundations and before long the house stood as it had long ago. Albeit the damage had been done and the house would never be the same. The front door was discernable, but large pieces of the exterior foundations had been taken by the woods, by nature itself. Half a house but it was once a complete home. The detailed carving on the front door was the only remaining piece of the house that any of them recognized. Walking through the remnants to the room that the twins had once shared the foursome moved slowly. The cold air combined with the rain began forming white flakes. The descending snow followed them as they congregated in the former room. The boys looked to each other and exchanged a quick smile. Looking down to the earthen floor, they took their fists and thrust them into the muddied ground. With each hit, a deeper hole was made. The earth being flung into the air about them had no impact on their goal. Eventually, mud soaked, the boys emerged holding a chest between them. They carried it out of the foundation and into the clearing. She and Patty looked on without a word. The chest was made of the most sustainable metal that could have been found. The lock was still in place, which was a good sign for all concerned. Patty stepped up between them. She looked up to the sky and watched each flake descend on them. Soaked through and covered in the layers of unearthed substance that had been used as an impenetrable safe, all held their breaths as Patty pulled at the lock with little to no effort. The lock responded to her touch and fell open. She knelt to the ground and slowly opened the chest. Within were the only remaining documents they needed. For so long, they had waited. The boys picked up the chest and returned to the house with the girls in tow. The four re-entered the basement while the girls wiped all traces of their visit as they tracked through the home. They walked back down the stone hall toward the cabin. Once there, they placed the chest in front of the fireplace and picked up their bags. The boys shut the entry door to the hall; all three picked up their bags and proceeded to ride back to the house rain soaked and mud covered. Birdie watched them ride through the trees and looked back at the chest. They had removed all the documents from the chest and re-locked it. She lit the fireplace for their return and retreated upstairs as the rain began to pour heavier from the sky.

Chapter Six

The tires of his car rolled on the gravel leading to the house. Right away, he noticed a difference. The tracked mud leading up to the house wouldn't be a second thought to someone in a neighborhood, but out in the sticks there was no reason someone would approach the house. He looked back toward the old highway and then back to the house. Following the trail to the front door, he slowly opened it.

Letting the door fall open, he paused. He moved slowly through the opening one foot then the other. The wood groaned beneath him and all in the house was quiet. He grinned as he looked to the floor. Spotless. Immaculate. He sighed. Moving into the kitchen the coffee cup sat by the sink. He inhaled and let his eyes wander to the living room. Slowly descending the stairs while still following the scent, he arrived in the basement. Taking in the emptiness of the room, he dropped his head to the floor. He placed his hands on the table and breathed in. He tilted his head toward the passage door. Walking down the hall, he hoped for good news. He placed the key in the lock, but the door made no response. The scent was stronger on the other side of the door. He pulled at the handle and the door came off its hinges.

Dirt and bits of stone came loose but he didn't care. He could just see them making their way to the far side of the trail. The table was filthy with the dust from his journals. He looked up at the lit fireplace and a smile began in the corner of his mouth and spread across his face as he slowly approached the chest. He looked back over his shoulder to the doorway leading to the lake. He had a good place to keep this until he needed it. He picked it up with no effort and carried it to the lakes edge. He stepped once more onto the edges of the lake and disappeared from view.

She walked down the stairs as he touched the lakes edge. Having heard him collect the chest from upstairs, she waited for his next move. While waiting for the weather to let up, she took the opportunity to look around the house. She looked through the rooms, bedside tables, dresser drawers, and closets to no avail. There was nothing of value left in the house. The sound of the lake bubbling caused her to turn and looking over her shoulder saw him emerging from the water. She took a chance and instead of retreating from the cabin toward the estate, she slowly walked toward the front door. He had a grin on his face and was looking at the ground as he approached the cabin door. He lifted his head as his foot touched the first step. There she stood by the table lit by the fire behind. His grin faded and was replaced by a brief glance of caution as to who all was inside. He stepped inside and shut the door. Looking left to right and glancing up at the stairwell, he made eye contact with her again. He sighed and approached her, causing her to walk backward until her back brushed against the wall adjacent to the mantle. She didn't look afraid or even worried, just curious.

"Is it just you?" he asked without emotion. She nodded. He stepped back and waited.

Putting his hands out in front of him, he gestured for her to begin. "How long have you been back?" she asked.

"Birdie, you can do better than that," he replied with disappointment.

"Where did you go?" she tried again.

"Everywhere" – he moved to the passage door – "Rome, Egypt, Tokyo, Mexico, you name it I went and visited, watched and waited for a reason to form in my head for what used to be my family to become nothing more than people that I associate no real emotion with. People who, for most of my life, cared for me, corrected me, uplifted me and with one night they became nothing, but people. Just people. People who live in this country, this state and no different than people who live in other countries, states, cultures, etcetera, etcetera." The passage door opened, and Richie appeared.

Drew gestured to Birdie, "So this happened." Richie nodded and moved toward the table.

"Did I miss anything interesting?" he asked looking from Drew to Birdie and back. Birdie felt her heart sink into her stomach as the realization hit.

"You knew he was back." She started slowly moving toward the front door. Richie raised his brows and dropped his gaze to the table.

"I've known where he was since he was born." Drew had begun walking down the hall back toward the house. Drew heard the scuffle between them but kept walking. Heard the window break, the table crash under the weight of something, but still he kept moving and once he reached the door he opened it, let it fall shut behind him as her loud scream reached his ears, "NO!" He retreated up the winding stair to his room and heard pots and pans in the kitchen. Following a shower, the scent of roast chicken greeted him and the faint sound of conversation. He dressed and made his way to the kitchen to find Richie and Agatha. The laughter dwindled when they saw him coming. "Hello, dear. You're just in time for dinner."

At Rachel and Jackie's Apartment

The girls tried on their dresses and found them to be perfect fits. Curious and extremely disturbing to Rachel, while Jackie couldn't stop admiring its twirl potential as well as her reflection in the mirror. Replacing the gowns in their respective closets Rachel set about making dinner for the two of them. "Chicken parm or lasagna?" she held up two frozen dinners and looked to Jackie.

"Uh, chicken please," came the response.

"How'd your meeting with Wendy go about changing your work schedule?" she asked while flipping through the channels for something to watch. The beeping and proceeding whirr of the microwave was followed by Rachel's retelling.

"I sat down in her office and she started re-listing the procedure for schedule alterations and I nodded and said I understood. Blah blah, it won't happen again, etc., etc. Then she started telling me how to date in a manner of speaking," she finished just as the microwave's three loud beeps foretold the chicken was done.

"What do you mean?" Jackie asked. Both now perched on the couch to watch TV as Rachel recalled the morning's meeting.

Earlier that morning.

Rachel arrived at the house for her meeting with Wendy, stepping off the Skyler bus with her coworkers. Making a beeline down the hall and past the kitchen, she took her seat in Wendy's office. Once there, Wendy reiterated the scheduling process as Rachel nodded. As she spoke, she began wondering why Rachel wanted to alter her schedule.

"Richie tells me you're seeing someone, and it is of no consequence to me, but I have seen over the years, women who work here tend to attract interested parties for the wrong reason. What I mean is—"

And Rachel tilted her head, pursed her lips and interrupted with, "You're right. It is of no consequence to you." Wendy wanted to make her point clear and persisted.

"Let me finish, please." Rachel rose from her seat, done with a lecture on her person choices.

"We've discussed the process for schedule alterations which I have stated was a mistake and accept your formal correction for it, but outside of work my choices are not under your umbrella of authority. I have put in for an adjustment the way it is meant to be done and now, if there is nothing else, I'm going to go about my workday." She stared calmly back at Wendy while her heart fought to come through her chest. Wendy leaned back in her chair and said, "Umbrella of authority," with raised eyebrows.

"No, that'll be all." Rachel left the room with as much calm as she could and proceeded up the stairs to start her day. Seeing her brush past the kitchen Reid made his way through the passage and up to the Skyler's. Seeing the whole family on the balcony caught him off guard.

"How many journals is that in total?" Fred asked. Rick was massaging his temples when he replied, "At least 80 that we could grab, but there have to be hundreds in that basement."

"And you left the chest in the cabin?" Fred asked. Rick nodded. "All we had were our bikes and we didn't know when he was coming back, if he uses the cabin or the lake…" And he trailed off.

"I get it. You said Birdie was with you. Morning, Reid," Fred greeted him offhandedly. Standing in the doorframe, Reid joined them on the balcony as Patty and Greg looked through what appeared to be extremely aged books at the table as Trish finished breakfast. Rick and Fred were lost in conversation at the balcony wall and Patty and Greg muttered their greetings without glances.

"Good morning, Reid, please join us." Trish gestured for him to sit. "Where is Birdie?" Trish asked of the group.

"She usually pops in to pick at some breakfast."

Rick turned to respond. "No idea. I'm sure she'll turn up." Fred checked his watch and made his way downstairs where Teddy was waiting with the car.

Back in Rachel and Jackie's apartment.

Jackie stared open mouthed, fork mid-air and asked, "Umbrella of authority?" She tilted her head to the side and began laughing. Rachel closed her eyes and fell into laughter.

"I don't know where I came up with the phrase, but I just wanted to get out of there and move on like it never happened." Rachel's phone buzzed and she reached for the coffee table.

"*Please report to Wendy's office tomorrow morning prior to beginning your shift*." Rachel sighed.

"Apparently not moving ahead."

Jackie furrowed her brows, "What is it?" Rachel shook her head and showed her the message.

The following morning, Rachel arrived at the house for her meeting with Wendy. Once in her office Wendy reiterated the previous day's conversation of the scheduling process as Rachel confirmed her understanding. Aware that she was having a completely redundant meeting, Rachel brought up the dresses.

"Jackie and I received the dresses for the fundraiser and they're beautiful, thank you. We were wondering how you knew our sizes because they fit perfectly." Wendy smiled.

"Only a few of the non-residential staff will be there and Mrs. Skyler has a good eye for that sort of thing."

"I'll be sure to send a thank you note." Wendy grinned but shook her head. "That won't be necessary as the dresses are actually on loan for the event itself and once over should be returned." Rachel raised her eyebrows.

"Okay," she slowly replied. That raised more questions than answers, but Wendy started in on the visit to the residential floor.

"For our records, this is a formal warning not to go up to the residence unless for work purposes." Rachel started sweating and could feel her heart racing in her chest. "Oh, yes of course. I am sorry about that."

"Now that's all sorted, be sure to drop by the kitchen for some breakfast."

Rachel nodded. Once in the kitchen, she seized upon eggs, bacon, and orange juice. The other staff members were engaged in various conversations and Jackie asked if she was alright. Rachel nodded.

"So, tomorrow night is the fundraiser. Who all is going?" Rachel asked the table. All conversation stopped. Maggie and Steven turned to look at Rachel with amusement.

"The fundraiser is for residential employees and Skyler guests only," came Maggie's reply. Rachel glanced around the table and then across at Jackie, who was beaming from car to ear. "Well, I guess that makes the two of us" – Jackie gestured between the two of them – "Skyler guests." Awash with confusion and excitement, the other employees began asking questions about the invite which Jackie was only too happy to discuss as well as describe the dresses they would be wearing. Breakfast drew to a close and the day went on as usual. Here and there, Rachel would bump into a coworker asking for details about the fundraiser. Rachel made the same reply each time, she knew as much as anyone else: nothing. She still had no idea what she was meant to do and by the time the day was over, she was relieved to see a missed text from Drew. *Dinner tonight?* Rachel smiled and confirmed. It would be nice to end the day on a normal note.

Once at the apartment, Rachel realized that Jackie had been talking the whole ride home. After a few 'uhuh's' and 'yeah's', she threw on some sneakers, a hoodie, and headed out to meet Drew for dinner. Driving to The Grill, Rachel let the car radio music overtake her.

Arriving at the restaurant and now singing acapella as she walked inside, the hostess greeted her. Rachel pointed over her shoulder to Drew seated in the bar. Joining him with a smile, he asked, "How was everything today?" Rachel sighed.

"It was same old same old. Had a meeting with Wendy to say once again, 'do not go up to the residential floor', and I said fine. I put in for a later shift like we talked about and then the day just sort of went by." Drew grinned.

"Those are the best days. So, are you excited for this masquerade party?" he asked. Rachel laughed and nodded.

"At first, I was excited, but now I'm getting a little nervous because it's not a party, it's a fundraiser that I'm not working at, but will be attending with my employers, coworkers, and a ton of well-funded people." The waitress brought the nacho appetizer by, and Rachel took a few chips and was lost in thought when Drew cleared his throat.

"Okay, your bosses, coworkers, and a bunch of rich people will all wear outdated clothes and hide their faces as if they're attending some sad college party. So what?" She shrugged and then she remembered Jackie was attending as well and her face lit up. Drew smiled and said, "Whatever just happened in your head didn't come out of your mouth." Rachel laughed and told him about Jackie going as well.

"I'm pretty sure it's just the two of us who were invited that are non-rez employees, but it'll be nice to not think about work and just enjoy the house for once." Drew clenched his jaw.

"Are you okay?" she asked.

"Yeah, I just respond poorly to my shin being slaughtered." He winced. Without realizing, Rachel had been kicking him under the table. Her mouth dropped open as her eyebrows shot up.

"Oh, my goodness! I am so sorry. I thought it was a table leg." Drew massaged his shin and reminded her that they were at a booth. Both fell into laughter.

The comedian took to the stage and their food came just as Drew's shin stopped throbbing. "How are you getting to the house tomorrow night, and do I need a pass or something to go?" he asked. Rachel had just taken a healthy bite of her cheeseburger and grinned. "Sorry." He laughed.

She smiled back and replied, "The bus is coming to our place to take us, as well as the employees working the event, so you can just park in the visitor spot at our complex." He nodded.

"Oh! I heard from someone today that they supply masks at the door for anyone who forgets." Drew laughed.

"That's good news as my zorro mask won't do for this type of gathering I don't think." She grinned.

"What are you wearing to the fundraiser?" she asked. His eyes grew dark, and a sly grin formed across his mouth.

"I was able to find something in my closet. It's a suit, but I'm pretty sure it'll blend in with the whole nineteenth-century attire that you told me about." She tilted her head.

"How do you know?"

"Gut feeling," he replied.

"Cool." She decided to let it go. She glanced at his necklace, and he followed her gaze.

"When I was cleaning the other day, I noticed that stone in some of the jewelry worn by the people in the paintings. One of the twins was actually wearing a cufflink that looks almost exactly like that." She gestured to Drew. He nodded and continued eating his wings.

"That's nice," he added. She squinted her eyes.

"You told me before that you were from here and I've noticed you have similar jewelry to them, that's a little bit more than a coincidence." She stared at him.

"People wear crosses, saints, stars, and the other day, I saw a guy wearing the eye of Horus. Similar doesn't mean the same. What's your actual question?" She sighed.

"Do you know the family? You asked quite a lot of questions about the house at first, which I thought was normal considering its old and secluded etc., but then you started asking about the family. The twins and their sister are all back and are attending this thing tomorrow with us." He pushed his plate away.

"The house is interesting, and I've heard my share of rumors about the family, but I'm not exactly on speaking terms with them. Seeing doesn't mean knowing and similarity doesn't mean familiarity." She sighed.

"Would you be interested in meeting them?" He tilted his head to the side and half smiled.

"I think that would be very interesting." The comedian had long since departed and a band had begun to play. The bar was becoming overcrowded and conversation almost impossible to hold. Rachel decided to call it a night. Drew walked her to her car outside and she gave him the address to the complex.

"I look forward to seeing you tomorrow evening." He hugged her and she reached up to kiss him. She met his lips for a moment and forgot the meetings with Wendy, awkward encounters with the family and the event tomorrow. For one moment, it was just her and Drew. She opened her eyes and pulled away. He looked into her eyes and kissed her on her forehead.

"See you tomorrow." He straddled his bike as she started her car, and they went their separate ways.

Arriving back at the complex, Jackie was finishing eggplant parm and saw the look on Rachel's face. "Wow. You good?" she asked. Rachel sighed.

"We kissed," she stated. No emotion, no excitement, just a statement. Jackie blinked.

"So not romantic then?" she raised her brows. Rachel squinted at the floor.

"As kisses go, not overly, no. But I just wanted to go for it. I mean we're not kids, but there's something about him and we've been on a few dates now and tomorrow he's going with me as my plus one. Who are you taking?" she asked. Jackie grinned from ear to ear.

"I asked Jordan if he could take one day from security stuff to go with me and Geoff approved it." Rachel smiled back at her.

Drew pulled up to his house and noted Richie on the front porch. Once inside the house, Drew settled into the couch in the family room. He could hear the dull flapping of what sounded like wings. He sighed as Richie sat in the chair opposite him.

"How is she?" he asked. Richie shook his head.

"I don't even want to look," Drew replied. He told Richie about the dinner with Rachel.

"A kiss? Why?" Richie wondered. Drew rolled his eyes.

"A final farewell I think," he said.

"For you or her?" Richie questioned. Drew grinned. "Tomorrow night should be interesting. I'm going to bed." Drew proceeded down the hall to his room and Richie moved toward the spiral stairwell leading to the basement. At the bottom of the stairs and atop the table, now cleared of books and dust, rested a birdcage with an agitated occupant. Richie moved toward the door and proceeded toward the cabin. His car waited just beside the lake, and he glanced at the waters, the cabin, and what little of the roof he could make out of the estate far off.

Chapter Seven

The morning of the fundraiser had dawned, and the house was in full chaos. Organized chaos, but chaos, nonetheless. Floral arrangements, ice sculptures, tents, table settings, security sweeps, and more all blew through the gates of the house and the staff were buzzing with excitement. The kitchen was overflowing with prep stations, the freezers were filled to capacity, and Wendy was busy reviewing the list of items she had ordered for the night's courses and glancing around the kitchen to account for all of it.

The morning staff were using the sideboard as a grazing station. Every so often, the kitchen door would swing open and a hand or two would find its way to the buffet style set up of plates, bacon, eggs, cinnamon rolls, fruits, etc., before immediately discarding an empty plate and returning to the day's activities. Once outside the kitchen door and down the hall, the staff were in full motion with paintings being swapped for more valuable ones to be shown off, circular tables being carried to the dining room along with electrical equipment for the auction set up and outside were fireworks displays in the beginning stages of establishment. Upstairs, the family were dispersed on the balcony as well as on the sofas just inside.

Reviewing the documents they had found in the chest, there was disappointment layered on each face. Fred had discarded his selected paper stack and stood with his back against the balcony wall and facing the family.

"The lock was the same one?" he asked. Rick's response was quick as he stood to approach the balcony. "Yes, the exact one. As you can see, the papers are—"

"Worthless," deadpanned Richie. "The first few sections were land deeds, certificates and I am pretty certain that this bunch here is complete gibberish," he said holding up a stack of papers with nonsensical writing and distorted letters written from top to bottom.

The whole family had now gathered on the balcony. Looking down to the firework setup below and then back to the family at large, Fred raised his eyebrows and sighed. "I'm not angry or anxious about this at all. The fact that he managed to, at some point" – he gestured to the papers strewn along the table – "switch out all of it for faded, irrelevant and" – nodding toward Richie – "nonsensical gibberish documents, is a little impressive. Was the chest?" he paused and seemingly stared off. The twins looked to each other.

"What?" they asked. Fred closed his eyes and started laughing. "Was the chest decorated in any way?" he asked with his eyes still closed. The twins looked more frustrated with the line of questioning. "No. It's metal on the outside and inside, just like it always had been," came Geoff's slow reply.

Trish registered what Fred was alluding first. "Was there a brand on its top?" he asked. The twins and Patty shook their heads. "It's been in the ground for however long and filthy as a result. Everything stuck to it as we pulled it up and carried it back to the cabin." Geoff pointed toward the lake.

"He switched them," muttered Richie. All eyes glanced to him and then to Fred.

"If you could please check if there is a brand on the chest, I would very much appreciate it," Fred spoke calmly. The twins and Patty turned and made their rapid exit toward the garage. Once on their bikes and much to the agitation of the bustling employees outside, they made their way to the cabin following the same path through the woods as before.

Richie remained with the Skyler's on the balcony and started laughing. Fred and Trish shook their heads. "If he switched them, then he has the book, the albums, the rock, the money, etc." Fred moved to leave, but Trish motioned for him to stop.

The trio had entered the cabin only to find the inside in complete disarray. The front window was broken, the table smashed in two and the chest gone. Looking to each other, they made their way to the tunnel door only to find it locked. Back on the balcony, Trish stood and shook her head. "The chest couldn't have been switched because the first wasn't big enough, but the other one…" she trailed off. Fred looked toward the lake.

"Had a false bottom," he finished. Richie moved into the house to help with the day's business while the Skyler's remained and waited for news from the trio.

Richie descended the stairwell to the first floor past fluid motions of window cleaners, stair sweepers, rug cleaners, florists, table movers, painting carriers, and the like until he arrived in the kitchen. Reid was just filling his plate with breakfast and Maggie was seemingly satisfied that all had arrived and in the right amounts for the night's festivities. Richie saw Rachel discarding her plate and moved to intersect her exit. "I heard you received an invite to the Foundation's dinner." Rachel swallowed the remainder of her breakfast and nodded. "Jackie and I have our dresses, dates and are happy to be going, but I do have to move past you, if you'll excuse me." Richie moved aside and Rachel made her way down the hall and up the stairwell surrounded by the buzzing activity of the house.

The second floor was just as swarmed as the first. Many of the employees Rachel saw for the first time as most were hired on as extra for prepping and then she assumed the same would occur this evening. Moving into the drawing room, she began vacuuming the rug while the window cleaners outside made quick work of their responsibility.

In the tunnel, Rick used his strength to break the door and emerged in the basement where they had previously found the journals. Much to Patty's surprise, the room was pristine. The table, floors, and now mostly empty bookshelves were immaculate. Moving upstairs to the main house, they heard voices in the kitchen followed by the opening and closing of the front door.

Greg led the trio through the house to see the car leaving the gravel drive through the front windows. The sound of claws against metal made them turn. Stepping further into the house, the sound of rustling feathers grew louder. Opening a door just past the bedroom they had seen previously was a small closet, just big enough to fit a cage on the floor beneath some shelving. Black feathers and blood were strewn around the outside of the cage itself and one of the wings was visibly damaged.

Rick picked up the cage and the trio sped back to the cabin. Once there, the cage was placed on the floor and the door opened. She hobbled out and collapsed on her belly onto the ground simultaneously transforming to her natural form. Her shoulder was visibly dislocated, her hand broken in two places and a sizeable wound to her forehead that had yet to stop bleeding. Greg picked her up and moved to take her to the lake as her eyes fell shut. Patty stopped him just as he reached the final step of the cabin.

"We don't know where he is." She pointed to the water. "It's better if we take her to Trish and let her rehab in the residence tonight then take a chance." Greg nodded. "Birdie, I need you to open your eyes." There was no response.

Patty became panicked. Rick took her from Greg. "I'll take her, you two get the bikes back to the garage and leave mine by the cabin. I'll come back for it." Rick sped effortlessly through the trees and along the path leading to the house leaving Greg and Patty with the bikes. Once in sight of the back of the house, he maneuvered just hidden by tree cover as the fireworks display being setup was still in full motion.

Holding Birdie in his arms, she let out a small groan. Rick sighed. He could just see Fred and Trish on the balcony. *Birdie's in bad shape.* Fred turned on the spot and looked into the tree line. Catching a small glimpse of Rick holding something across his arms, he checked his watch and turned to enter the house as the car would be waiting for him at the front door to take him to work. Once inside, he ran into Reid. "After you take the tray down to the kitchen, be sure to stop by the security floor. Trish will meet you there." Reid nodded.

Trish was looking into the far side of the tree line now toward the garage as Rick waited for a lull in the workers. Reid joined her on the balcony and followed her gaze. Seeing an opportunity, Rick advanced unseen toward the corner of the house and pushing one of the stones on the wall, an entry way opened, and the two of them slipped in. Trish made her way to the elevator and Reid to the kitchen. Once on the security floor, the doors opened to a flurry of activity.

There was a crowd of employees outside the infirmary down the hall from the security office. Several of the security team had alerted Geoff to Rick's use of the hidden entryway. Most of the team had ventured out to the foyer to see the commotion. "How long has she been unconscious?" asked Geoff. Hearing the question through the door, Trish advanced through the parting sea of employees through to the infirmary. An IV was being prepared for Birdie as Rick was placing her on the bed. Reid came through the painting down the hall and proceeded to the infirmary. Seeing Birdie for the first time, Trish's eyes became wide, and the sky outside became black followed by thunder and lightning in the distance. Geoff motioned for more gauze as Reid took his place beside Trish.

"Ten minutes at most," came Rick's reply. Trish motioned for Geoff to move aside as she moved to set Birdie's shoulder. Rick stood back and Geoff began questioning him. A small groan escaped Birdie's lips as she thrashed from the pain. Trish looked to her hand and made quick work of it. With one arm in a sling, an I.V. started and a thick bandage over her eye, Birdie drifted off.

"You said she was in the closet," Geoff asked. Rick nodded as Reid shook his head. He looked at Birdie on the bed and noticed the shadows outside the infirmary had begun to fade as the team had gone back to work. "She was in the cage on the floor of the closet. I don't know how long she had been there. The cabin itself looked like a wrecking ball had landed inside it. The tunnel leading to that house is old and I don't know when that was done and why we never knew of it, but I don't see a way this ends well for him."

Geoff motioned for them to move the conversation to the foyer. Once in the foyer, Geoff motioned for them to sit. "I have security looking into the cabin as we speak. The tunnel seems to be as old as this place." He motioned around him.

"The old house he's in right now is a foreclosure so it's been sitting for a while and no reason anyone would check on it." Trish cleared her throat.

"Why would he attack her? She's never done anything to anyone. It doesn't make sense, not to mention the violence and cruelty." She motioned toward the infirmary. Rick spoke up next.

"Well, he's not unaccustomed to cruelty and violence. So, if we're looking for a logical explanation for this, I think that's a wasted effort." Reid spoke for the first time.

"I understand that his temper and actions have a history as you guys have shared with me in the past, but the extent of it, now? I agree with Trish. It doesn't make sense for him to have done this." The group was still in session when the painting swung open revealing Richie with a face full of concern.

Out of breath, he ran toward the foyer. "What happened?" he exclaimed. "I overheard some of the security team muttering about Birdie. Is she alright?" he asked. Trish rose and embraced him.

"She's in the infirmary. We still don't know why he would have ever done this. It doesn't make sense. It's so random and brutal." Richie turned to head down the hall.

"What do you mean brutal? What happened?" He proceeded down the hall and with his back to the family still in talks his face of concern turned to one of indifference.

He pushed open the door of the infirmary and spoke under his breath, "I'd like to thank the academy." Walking toward the curtained bed containing Birdie, he was prepared for a final act. He opened the curtain and saw her lying there. He replaced the curtain around them and sat on the bed.

"Wrong place, wrong time as usual for you." He moved a stray piece of hair off her face. The door swung open revealing Greg and Patty, faces filled with anxiety and worry. Quickly rising and opening the curtain, he greeted them with hugs and words of empathy. "Was Trish able to help?" Patty asked. Richie nodded and moved away from the bedside. Greg and Patty sat on either side of Birdie.

"We just finished talking with Geoff. He's never been like this before. Even years ago. Remember the night you walked in?" Greg asked and looked to Patty.

"That night is always going to be a bit of blur for me, but staggering as opposed to walking in, is what I remember and to answer your question, even then he wasn't physically cruel. He's more of a mental terrorist than anything else," she responded. Richie's face remained fixed.

Birdie let out a small groan. Richie cleared his throat. "Given the extent of her injuries I think it would be best if she were to be left to rest in peace." The two nodded and as they left the room.

"I'll leave you with her," Greg said. Watching the door swing shut, he turned once more to the bed. He was inches away from placing his hand across her mouth and nose when the door swung open once more leaving him to brush a hair off her forehead as Reid approached.

"They all want to see you in the foyer," he said.

"Of course," he replied and followed him out. In the foyer, the family had begun discussing the fundraiser.

Bristling with frustration, Richie listened as Geoff rattled on about tonight's security changes and watched as the family soaked it all in. Reid listened as this would be the first time he would be attending in any capacity. He watched Richie and noticed something was off. Richie had seen Fred head off to work and was patiently waiting for this tirade to be over when the infirmary door slowly opened. Richie turned to see Birdie stumbling through the frame with one hand on the IV pole and her other side leaning on the frame. The group swiftly moved to help her.

She had been glancing down to the floor and with Richie being the first to her aid she looked up to him and her eyes rolled back before saying, "Richie, no," in a whisper. Placing her back on the bed, Trish had previously given her an exam and didn't find any signs of a concussion and gave her some pain meds to help her sleep and recuperate. With Fred on his way into work, Birdie incapacitated but just down the hall from the security team and the house filled with to do lists, they all resumed their daily activities if only to attempt a sense of normality. Richie gave her one last look before leaving and joined the rest of the world upstairs.

The buses for the next group of employees had begun to arrive as the morning had flown by. Work for the night had become even more feverish. As tents had started being set up on the front lawn and chairs under the same, a side table in preparation for drinks was being set up as well. Rachel and Jackie boarded the bus and noted the intermittent lighting being set up along the drive for the night's guests that would be seeing the house that evening.

Coming into town, the stress and rapid workflow of the day drifted off. The complex had just come into view and Jackie was abuzz with questions about tonight's events. The leaflets in their seat backs had told them the buses would arrive at 8:30 to pick them up, nothing would be required of them in terms of work and any dates that required a jacket, or mask would be provided if requested. All plus ones were required to attend with their date and could not arrive alone. There were no exceptions. With a few hours to go before they had to start getting ready, Rachel wanted to take a power nap. No sooner had she started climbing the stairs to their apartment, than Jackie shouted from her car, "Rachel, where are you going? We have appointments." Rachel turned on the spot.

"Appointments?" she questioned back. Descending the stairs to Jackie's car, she squinted her eyes. Jackie looked back at her as though Rachel had been struck on the head.

"Ya know that thing we're going to tonight where our bosses and a lot of influential people will be?" she asked.

Rachel stood at the passenger door. "Yeah."

"Well, I made appointments for us to get our nails and hair done for it. I noted that on the guest list was the head of HR for the foundation itself. Did you also know that their head of art acquisitions is attending?"

Rachel smiled. "I'm sensing a pattern here."

"Oh good, I thought I was being too subtle. You have an art history degree and ton of retail experience. You're holding a door frame position right now, but if you can make small talk with the right people tonight you may get yourself through the door and." She trailed off and started the car as Rachel sat down opposite her.

"A potential job in the art department doing something that requires my academic interests," she finished.

"Hmm imagine that." Jackie raised her brows and turned on the radio.

Rachel smiled and shook her head. "Are you done?"

Jackie responded, "Mhm."

At the salon, Jackie had specific requests in place. As she was making detailed requests about their hairstyles, Rachel just closed her eyes and thought back on the kiss at the restaurant. *Drew seemed indifferent that night which meant the relationship experiment was done, but it's nice to have someone to go with tonight that isn't work related. Richie had spoken to me randomly, again, and no one else seems to be invited. What is so different about this year?* The lull of conversation from Jackie was interrupted by the stylist handing them each a mirror to look at their hair. *Wow,* thought Rachel. Half up and held together with untold numbers of pins, her hair had been curled and styled just off the shoulder and sprayed within an inch of its life. Normally, Rachel had a wash and wear hair routine that involved ponytails, but this was a look she couldn't have imagined. Jackie was admiring herself and after complimenting each other, they thanked their respective stylists and left for their next appointment. Rachel checked her phone and they had been in there for an hour and a half. The nail salon was next on the list and would only take half an hour. Rachel wasn't fond of dressing up and would rather be outside running marathons, reading under trees, going to the movies and the like. This day would be all the more tedious if not for Jackie.

Pulling up to the salon, the goal was a simple manicure, no fake nails, no designs, no neon colors, just clean and simple. Jackie asks for white tips and after half an hour, they were on their way back to the complex with an hour to spare before Drew would be showing up.

Once inside their apartments, they made beelines for their rooms and dresses. Taking hers out of the garment bag and off the hanger, Rachel put it on and looked in her bathroom mirror for the first time. It didn't have that over the top, huge skirt, but still maintained that vintage appeal with lace trimming on the elbow sleeves, neckline and the trim around the floor of the skirt. Pale pink from head to toe, wasn't the color she would have chosen right out the gate, but it surprised Rachel how nice it all had come to together as she looked in the mirror. The sash around the waist was a darker shade of pink with lace embroidery on it. The whole thing looked so precisely attuned to that era, almost like it was pulled from a history book. She couldn't help but think of the pictures in the residence of the family and their clothes and how similar this dress was to them. She walked out of her room to find Jackie twirling in front of the TV. Her blue dress had the same design elements, and her face was filled with excitement.

Chapter Eight

A knock on the door startled them both. Jackie answered it, revealing both Jordan and Drew. The boys entered holding their masks. Jordan's suit was simple and would have resembled a tuxedo if not for the long tie instead of a bowtie. Drew, on other hand, looked as though he stepped out of a costume store. His over coat had a short cloak, making it look like a cape. The four of them eyed each other up. "I think we look amazing!" squealed Jackie. She embraced Jordan, who looked more than a little uncomfortable.

"Still not sure why we're going to this. It's going to be so weird," Jordan said pulling at his tie. "You look beautiful, Jackie." She smiled and thanked him.

"You look really good. I've only seen you in uniform or work out gear." She smiled. Jordan grinned. The buses would be arriving in a few minutes, so the group began moving toward the bus pick up.

On their walk, Drew complimented Rachel, "You look stunning. Almost out of a movie." Rachel laughed.

"Thank you. I was thinking that it looked so realistic. I'm pretty sure this is real lace." She ran her fingers over the neckline's trim.

Drew grinned. "They probably had someone make them." Rachel hadn't thought of that. Boarding the bus with employees eyeing them and grinning from ear to ear, Rachel began to feel self-conscious. As Jordan took his seat behind Drew and Rachel, the rest of the employees began to whistle at him. Jordan laughed.

"It'll be nice to eat fine food, drink nice wine, and dance with our bosses, while you guys are patrolling outside, getting bit by mosquitoes, eating" – and he turned to look behind him and saw some of the guys eating jerky – "well, eating that." He turned back around in his seat and heard the expletive responses and laughed. Jackie was practically bouncing in her seat. Drew and Rachel maintained a steady silence as she looked out the window as the bus approached the estate. A long line of cars from a diverse range of companies had begun lining the route up the house. As they sat in the queue, the procession moved slowly. The drive was lit on either side by lamps that wound along the road up the main house. Once there, the clear tent in front of the house sheltered chairs and a cocktail table for the fireworks later on. The steps leading into the house were flanked with oversized floral displays and the interior of the house had transformed into a conservatory unto itself. Littered throughout the displays were twinkle lights as guests meandered through to the dining room. Once off the bus, the four donned their masks and made for the entrance, where Richie was waiting with a list of guests. Richie asked them to remove their masks. Having noticed two men being carted off by police as the bus pulled up, Jordan questioned Richie about it. "Small time art thieves." He showed a clipboard with a list of names with corresponding photographs of guests and another with the same except the names corresponded to thieves.

"How do you know they're small time?" Jackie asked. Richie motioned to Jordan. Richie checked off their names and they reapplied their masks. As they walked in and Jackie took in the wonder around her, Jordan began explaining.

"Whenever they throw these things, the police get a list of known offenders together and cross reference them with the area and then they give that list with pictures, to Richie."

"I thought there were some who managed to get through a few years back?" she asked. Jordan nodded.

"Those two coordinated with a vendor to help set up the displays. They applied to work under false names and, well you saw how many people were here today, it was chaos. Anyway, the two of them planned to take one of the paintings from its frame on the night of the event. They were posing as wait staff and earlier in the day had moved some of the floral displays in front of a painting. They waited for everyone to move into the gala room upstairs and made for the painting, believing that the floor would be deserted, and all focus would be elsewhere. They got the painting off the wall and had just begun to remove it from the frame," Jackie interrupted.

"How were they planning to walk away with a multi-million-dollar painting?" she asked.

"Getting there. They were removing the painting from the frame when Reid came in with Richie. Both of whom just stared at them. The story goes that Richie approached the two and said, 'Oh I see. Thank you. I wondered about the stability of that one in particular. Here let me help you put it back in its place. Oh, and the frame seems to need repair as well. Good catch boys.' By then, a couple of security guys had walked in as well and the two thieves made for the door where Geoff and a police car were quietly waiting outside. They didn't know about the camera in the corner of that room or that once everyone is upstairs the security team more or less fans out more deliberately through the house and a buffet of food unattended cannot be ignored. The security guys that had followed Reid into the room with Richie were actually enjoying some chicken when the thieves bolted for the door. One of the thieves had a small duffle bag with him and they had planned to fold the painting, stash it in the bag, and walk out the delivery entrance after the gala." Jackie smiled.

"I remember now. The vendor had company bags for the electric equipment with the company's logo on it. The two had come in, set up lighting, and placed that bag in one of the potted plant vases for later that night." Jordan nodded.

"Richie and Reid adjusted the frame and put the painting back on the wall, so by the time everyone came back downstairs for the front lawn fireworks, the thieves had been quietly managed, and no one was the wiser. The security cameras had the whole thing on tape and so there was no need to make a big show of force." Jordan and Jackie found their table in the dining room and took their seats as Rachel and Drew approached Richie.

As the queue of attendees began to grow, employees assisting with the check-in could be heard reminding guests not to put their masks on until they had been inside. Rachel motioned to Drew. "Richie, this is my date, Drew." Richie looked with indifference at him and looked to the list of guests in his hand. Marking a check next to Rachel's name and the 'plus one', he gave a polite smile and they entered. Drew grinned and put his mask back on. Crossing the threshold of the house, Drew took a deep breath in. Rachel looked to him, "Are you okay?"

"Hmm? Yes. It just looks so different from the pictures I've seen online." He smiled. He began looking around and taking in the space in front of him. Rachel did likewise and was overwhelmed with the florals, lighting, and paintings that she could only remember seeing in documentaries.

"It's beautiful, isn't it?" she asked.

"It's certainly well maintained." He gestured to the plastic overlay on the walls and glanced around the room subtly taking in the number of security cameras as they progressed. Rachel nodded.

"The wallpaper is original or as close to it as they could get as time has gone on, according to the tour guides," she replied. Walking through the wealth of blooms, they made their way to the dining room. Circular tables had been placed throughout the room from end to end as a fire roared on the wall and the windows on the wall opposite provided a clear view of the night sky.

Each table had fine white linen, gold-bordered plates and glass ware from an earlier age. The guests had finally all made their way to their respective tables. In the center of the room was the widest oval table for the family to be seated. The far two double doors opened as the family made their way in to join the dinner. Fred and Trish were glancing around the room and smiling at guests as they went. The two of them wore period pieces that looked right out of a movie. Trish's purple dress was pristine with black embroidered lace around her waist, neckline, and the skirt edge. Greg, Rick, and Patty joined soon after with similar attire, but Patty's dress was eye catching in its pale blue sheen and white sash around the waist instead of lace. The sash had no detailing on it and the dress held no lace. Her mask was pale blue with a white border. The family took their seats, and the dinner was well underway with Jackie narrating her thoughts on everyone in the room.

"Oh wow!" Jackie said so the four of them could hear. She was looking at Patty. Jordan rolled his eyes and took a sip of water. Drew had watched like a hawk as the family walked to the table and noted Patty's dress. He cast a side glance to Richie standing along the wall, who grinned back at him. Apart from the different sash, the five of them looked exactly as they had that night.

Drew noted that their table was seated in relatively close proximity to the family. Richie had told him that the family wanted to use Rachel has bait. He had just managed to tune out Jackie's incessant rambling when dessert was served, and she started up again. *Good gracious, she's a live version chatty Cathy doll,* he thought. Richie grinned as did the Skyler's before all of them tensed up and taking turns made side glances at the table. He glanced at Rachel as she finished her dessert. He noted with a grin that when she enjoyed something she was eating she would hum slightly, just under her breath.

Little by little, the tables were emptying out and guests began venturing upstairs. The Skyler's began mingling with everyone as they made their way. The stairwell had been wrapped in floral vines and the windows along it showed a clear skyline of the town at a distance and nothing but forest between. As the four climbed the stairwell, Jordan noted the security team doing sweeps with some looking up at the guests and finding Jordan's eye, were given an ear-splitting grin. The room itself was used as a multipurpose area during the year. The foundation had dividers that they would install and have different historical displays about the family in different subdivided rooms. To see the room in its open nature was a sight to behold.

The old oak floors laid a firm foundation for the sharp heels, dress shoes and glass topped iron tables. Interspersed throughout the room were displays of causes: forest conservation with images of the family going back a century, coastal conservation to prevent erosion on the shores accompanied with images of the first settlers coming off ships. The people were difficulty to identify, but there was something familiar about the woman standing on the pier. Looking at the forest conservation table, the woman appeared there as well, holding a bird by its neck as others traipsed through the tree line. *The woman looked so familiar*, Rachel thought. The other tables had to do with building conservation to preserve historical sites like the church, the hospital, banks, etc., and were also littered with family images. The woman featured prominently in all of them, and she seemed close to a man in each of the photographs whose face was always turned away.

The list of items for the silent auction was posted on the wall at the head of the room. One of the items that caught her eye was the journal of Clara Barton chronicling her time in the civil war, so said the summary. *How in the world would they have been able to find that?* she thought. The room was brimming with bright florals and delicate lighting that made the space look enchanted. As the auction began and people took their seats at varying tables, Rachel began to feel a little lightheaded. She reached for her water and took a sip. *So many people in one space*, she thought, *the heat was getting to her*. The foundation's attendants began taking the boxes away from the conservation tables in order to count donations. The Skyler's joined the fray shortly thereafter and were subtly eyeing the room for Rachel and her plus one. Rachel had begun sweating and rose in order to find a restroom to splash some water on her face. Items such as a grandfather clock, a tour of the private parts of the house, a grand piano and more were being ticked off the list one by one.

Rachel made her way to the restroom and could barely focus on herself in the mirror. She clumsily splashed water on her face and reached for some paper towels. Standing upright and looking in the mirror, she saw standing behind her the woman from the photographs in the auction room. She blinked several times and breathed deeply. Opening her eyes, the woman was gone. She made her way back to the auction room and rejoined the table.

Drew leaned in. "Are you alright?" Rachel nodded, but still felt a little adrift. The journal was up next, and the chair of the nursing association made quick work of raising her paddle to acquire it. Rachel began feeling worse and asked Drew to help her downstairs to get some air. Making their way downstairs, Drew adjusted their route and made for the hall toward the planning office. Rachel was having trouble keeping up, but Drew held her steady. Passing the kitchen and the office, they turned to enter the painting of the lake. Rachel tripped slightly as they went through, but Drew picked her up with ease. Down the stairwell and to the security foyer they ran into Richie. He looked frustrated.

"Security is too tight." He glanced toward the infirmary. "I've looked through the residential rooms, the safe, the security team's office as a last resort and still come up empty." Drew held tight to Rachel who glanced up at Richie.

"Why?" Richie gestured to Rachel. Drew smiled down at her.

"Rick likes her. He may be more inclined to help if he can be the knight in shining armor." He moved toward the wall adjacent to the elevator and pushed revealing the hidden entrance used by Rick earlier. He carried Rachel through and used his speed to breeze through the tree line and back to the cabin. Richie rolled his eyes and sighed.

"This is becoming tedious."

Upstairs, the auction had come to a close and guests began descending the stairs and making their way to the front lawn for the fireworks. Jordan and Jackie noticed their counterparts leave the table and not return. Jordan also took note of Richie being gone. Once downstairs, Jordan didn't see any security guards and, on the lawn, he relaxed as he saw a few security lurking around the corners of the house seeming as subtle as possible. Still, something didn't feel quite right.

"Where did they go?" Jackie asked. "Is she alright? I should have gone with her. She doesn't know him that well." She glanced around nervously trying to find Rachel in the group assembled. Richie appeared behind the Skyler's as they made their way out to the lawn. Watching the guests mingle under the tent and seeing the clear sky overhead, the family dispersed among them.

"Well, that went seamlessly," Richie spoke to Fred. Fred smiled to a guest across the way.

"I haven't seen him and only heard him for a split second during the auction. I don't see the girl here. Where is she?" he asked. Richie looked through the assembly.

"I don't see her," he replied. Reid came out to the lawn, one hand in his pocket and his mask pulled up. He had been in the infirmary with Birdie most of the night but wanted to come out for the fireworks. Richie perked up.

"Oh, there you are!" He smiled. "I'll look around out here and inside if anyone has seen her."

Reid joined Fred and Trish under the tent while the hot cider and an assortment of other small items and drinks were being doled out. As the fireworks display was getting closer, several guests were taking selfies of themselves with their dates in front of the house. Richie made quick work of his search and made his way inside. Reid took note of Richie's re-entry to the house and grinned. Making his way back down to the infirmary, Richie slowly opened the door and approached the curtain drawn bed. Moving the cover aside, he found the bed empty. He clenched his jaw and turned slowly, perusing the room. He found the place empty and made his way to the cabin in frustration. Arriving at the lakes edge, he looked back through the tree line feeling as though he had been followed. He shook his head at the thought. Inside the cabin, Rachel was lying on the floor and Drew was sipping some cider watching the flames in the fireplace. Richie tutted.

"Drew," he said flatly, "the least you could do is prop her up in a chair or place her in one of the beds upstairs." Drew removed his mask, having forgotten it was on, and looked down at Rachel who was listing her head from side to side.

"Hmm, oh sure. Forgot she was there." He sighed. He lifted her with one arm and placed her over his shoulder taking her upstairs. Richie turned toward the front door knowing the fireworks would start any second. Drew placed her on the bed upstairs and returned to find Richie drinking the second glass of cider that he had left on the mantle.

"That's not for you." He grinned. Richie raised his brows.

"She's late, she doesn't get any cider," he responded. "We have another problem. Birdie is missing. I went to look for her in the infirmary and she was gone." Drew made his way out to the porch and along the lakes edge. He looked to the tree line surrounding the lake and back to the house and saw nothing out of the ordinary. *She's like a cockroach. She survived the hurricane in 1812, she's probably – I can't make myself care more than that.* He turned to look at the cabin, noting the footprints the security team had left from their earlier sweep.

He moved upstairs to raise the alarm. *Here we go,* he thought. He lit a candle on the bedside table as Rachel continued to let out little moans. Letting his guard down, he closed his eyes and exhaled. Opening his eyes once more and looking down at Rachel his thought echoed through the cabin, trees and up to the house. *She looks so peaceful here.* Richie looked up to the room and grinned. Within an instant, the wind tore through the trees and lightning struck around the lake. Fred was the first to appear, followed quickly by the family. Hints of smoke could be seen coming off Greg's shoulders and Trish's eyes had gone completely white as the wind began to die down. As Fred approached the lake the lightning subsided, and Rick approached the cabin. Patty's skin was turning a paler shade of white, and ice appeared with every step she took. Entering the cabin, they found the fire extinguished, window broken as before, and the table shattered. Dark and cold with nothing but their senses to guide them. Patty was standing on the porch and heard a sigh from behind her.

Standing on the lakes edge, Drew looked up at her. He smiled as her body turned to ice and she approached him. Rick saw him from the window frame and launched himself at Drew. Drew and Rick flew across the lake with Drew colliding with a tree with a resounding CRACK! Trish made her way up the stairs to find Rachel, but the bed was empty. Closer to the tree line by the house Rachel was being placed on the ground just on the outskirts of the water.

Drew and Rick continued their brawl as Fred saw the first of the fireworks explode into the air reflecting across the water. Seeing Rachel at the edge, Patty made her way over to her. "Rachel! Rachel!" She began to sit up and felt disoriented. Out of the tree line, came Richie. Patty breathed a sigh of relief. "Richie, take her up to the house. He's here. Rick and Greg are going to kill him!" He looked across the water and saw the commotion of trees falling and small fires roaring to life and then extinguishing in an instant. Patty followed his gaze and looked to him.

Richie looked down at Patty and said, "Well we can't have that now, can we?" He tilted his head. She furrowed her eyebrows and stood slowly facing him. More fireworks erupted in the sky and highlighted the trees around the lake in various hues of red, oranges, and greens. He picked Rachel up, setting her on her feet. Fred and Trish watched Richie as Rachel began regaining her senses. The fight across the lake had taken a turn as Rick was seen flying through the air and crashing into the trees. Greg was next as a fireball made its way in the same pattern. Richie wrapped his arm around her waist and placed his hand under her jaw.

"When was the last time you saw the rock, Patty?" he spoke softly. Patty stood frozen to the spot as Fred and Trish looked on. Fred took a step forward and Richie tightened his grip on Rachel's throat. The ground beneath them began to tremble and break. Richie smiled.

"I wouldn't," he said. The boys saw what was happening from across the water and Drew emerged from the tree line covered in dirt, scrapes, and what looked to be a dislocated shoulder. The twins had gashes across their faces and arms. Rachel looked over to them and couldn't believe what she saw. The twins' injuries had begun to heal as they stood there watching them and the lakes edge began to bubble as their feet touched it. Richie asked his question again. Patty shook her head. The night had continued on, but their surroundings were as bright as mid-day owing to the fireworks.

Fred and Trish made the same gesture. Rachel began to feel the pressure build in her head and her vision became spotty. From behind Richie, the sound of feet pounding into the ground was heard. Reid and Jordan came through the woods and Richie threw Rachel from him. She flew through the air and landed on the ground with her head hitting a rock with a resounding THUD! She could barely open her eyes as she felt warm liquid run over her eyes and down into her mouth. The taste of blood covering her lips and the sounds of shouting as she attempted to rise and failed.

Richie had vanished in the blink of an eye. Reid was brandishing a dagger and Fred took note of it. "Grace left that for you?" he asked. Reid nodded.

"She left me a DVD of instructions," he said trying to catch his breath. The fireworks were almost over and the twins had joined the others just as Richie disappeared. Rachel looked at the group and could feel the cold ache in her head. She thought back to seeing the twins and watching them heal. The last fireworks were sounding in the sky and the family had begun racing over to get to Rachel. She forced herself to stand and collapsed and forced herself again and again until he stood doubled over at the lakes edge and the sound of the last firework startled her into looking up and across the lake, she saw a woman standing between Drew and Reid. She took a step forward and the iciness of the water overcame her, and she collapsed into it. The family reached her just as the water enveloped her and took her under. Rick watched on in horror as did the family and Reid. They looked across the lake and saw the three of them standing there with grins on their faces. Fred's jaw dropped open when he recognized the woman. The trio entered the lake as its surface had begun bubbling with force. The twins and Patty couldn't believe their eyes.

"Grace?" Fred whispered.

Printed in the USA
CPSIA information can be obtained
at www.ICGtesting.com
LVHW011106051124
795747LV00013B/494